THREE TIMES A WOMAN

Katerina eyed her find with growing satisfaction. She went around and around the nude girl. The waistline was perfect; the legs full and female but subtle and the flesh of the arse seemed to be even softer than that of her mistress. To find out, she came close to the girl and felt her body. She was content. This was not the usual peasant type. This was not a tough and common brat. This girl had the form of an aristocrat. Katerina had already resolved that this girl was to be bought.

Starting towards the palace, Katerina asked the dark girl what her name was. 'Grushenka', answered the girl, readily. That was the first word she spoke after she had become one of the uncounted souls of Prince Alexey Sokolow.

THREE TIMES A WOMAN

Anonymous

A STAR BOOK
published by
the Paperback Division of
W. H. ALLEN & Co. PLC

A Star Book
Published in 1984
by the Paperback Division of
W. H. Allen & Co. PLC
44 Hill Street, London W1X 8LB
Reprinted 1984, 1985, 1988

This edition copyright © Star Books 1984

Printed and bound in Great Britain by
Cox & Wyman Ltd, Reading, Berkshire

ISBN 0 352 31460 5

CHAPTER I.

Katerina walked in great dismay through one of the unpaved streets in the Northerly quarter of Moscow. She had much reason to be uneasy and in bad humour. Here it was spring; soon the whole household would be moved to the country and she had not yet been able to fulfil the command of her mistress, the young and capricious Princess Nelidowa Sokolow. At first the Princess Nelidowa had only mentioned her request casually, as something she would like to have. But lately she had demanded, nay commanded. The young Princess had become very irritable. She was always on the go, never at rest, not even for a reassuring prayer.

It was not for Katerina to question the orders of her mistress. She was the housekeeper, an old and trusted serf, hardened by rough work, now burdened with the weight of running the huge household, to which the young and pleasure seeking Madame gave never a thought. She had been trained since her early youth to follow orders and to do so promptly. Katerina was not in dismay because she was afraid she would be punished. She was not in fear of the lash. No, it was not that. She simply wanted to do her duty and her duty was to satisfy her Lady.

What Princess Nelidowa wanted was this: a serf-girl, who had exactly her own measurements, who duplicated exactly her own figure. It may seem strange that Nelidowa should have had such a desire, but it was not. It must be imagined through what nerve-racking torture (so she thought at least) Nelidowa had to go standing as a model for hours and hours in her boudoir, while the tailor, the chemise-maker, the bodice-maker, the shoe-maker, the coiffeur and all the other untold clothiers tinkered around

1

her body.

Of course, it is every woman's delight to adorn herself, to choose and to invent what is most becoming to her. But Nelidowa was suddenly in a hurry. In a hurry to live, to enjoy herself, to play the lady, to be everywhere, to be seen, and last but not least, to be adored. To be adored and envied by women, meant clothes and more clothes. And that meant to have to stand still and suffer, to be touched all over by the dirty hands of the dress-makers. The Princess despised the dress-makers as she did all other working people and treated them haughtily and unjustly. She disliked the smell of them, but she had to bear it in order to look lovely and rich.

Rich! That was the word which sang always in the ears of the newly wed Princess. Rich, mighty, a figure at the court, a mistress of many souls. Of course there was a price to be paid for it, a price with disgusting features. This price was that she had to be the wife of Alexey Sokolow. She hated it, but what could she do? It was a bargain she could not confide to her most intimate friends. She was always conscious why she had to endure it, but had not thought yet how she might get round it.

For Nelidowa had been terribly poor. So poor that in the convent where she had been brought up, she had not been given enough to eat. The nuns had used her as a kitchen maid and on the great holidays, when all the other aristocratic girls donated candles to the Saints as big as a log, she could not even buy a little waxen stick. Her father had been a great general, a superb aristocrat, her mother a Tartar Princess. But when her father, in one of his usual drinking spells, had fallen into the Volga and drowned, his family was left without a penny. Ill-meaning relatives scattered his brood, as they called it, into institutions and charity houses.

Grown to be twenty, and without any desire to become a nun, an old and half blind aunt in a little city had taken her in. There she was chained to a cranky invalid who gave her the switch once in a while, which it was then the mode to use even for educated girls as long as they were not

2

married. Therefore, it was like a miracle when the match with the mighty Alexey Sokolow was suddenly in the air. It was a fata morgana, not to be trusted, and when it finally became true, Nelidowa had to pinch herself many times to make sure she was not dreaming.

This match had been made, after the fashion of the times, by correspondence. Now, in the little city where Nelidowa then lived, was a fickle young man, son of the Military commander of the district. He fell so violently in love with Nelidowa that he told his father—and told him with passion—that he was going to marry the girl of his love, although she was poor and socially a nobody. The father, as it goes in the world, did not want to consent. The best thing therefore, so it seemed to him, would be to remove the girl from the sight of his son and the best way to remove her was to marry her off. Being a school chum of the mighty Prince Alexey Sokolow, and having corresponded with him for many years, he now sent him such showers of praise about the virtue and charm of Nelidowa, that he succeeded in getting the old bachelor engaged to the girl by mail.

There was no doubt that Nelidowa would grasp this opportunity with all her ten nimble fingers. Ex-Governor Prince Alexey Sokolow, was known throughout the country as one of the richest landowners, a figure at court, a political factor and as a host who gave elegant parties. One of the grandees of his time, he had inherited his fortunes and tripled them by bold strokes which often bordered on robbery. That he was thirty-five years her senior did not disturb Nelidowa. It all meant one great windfall of luck for her. But that he consented to marry her made her wonder very much.

It cannot be said whether Sokolow would have been able to get one of the rich ladies of the court as a wife, but it is sure that he had his special reasons for making the abrupt decision to marry the unknown girl. These reasons were not that she was an aristocratic girl and the daughter of an old friend of his. No, the real reason was that Sokolow wanted to do some spite work to his relatives. They were already counting on his death, had already figured out what they would inherit from him, would in fact have liked to poison him. Now let them wail! He would marry this girl who was young and healthy, marry her and have children and the whole chorus of loving relatives would have to go away empty handed.

When this clever idea entered his head, he acted with his usual abruptness. Nobody should know beforehand. He simply wrote a letter to Nelidowa, without any explanations or previous correspondence, to the effect that he had heard from his old friend that she was a marriageable person, that enclosed were 5000 rubles for her dowry, that the ring he was sending had been worn by his mother, that the carriage sent to her door was hers, and that he expected her without fail by return post. But he advised her to travel by easy stages, so that she should not be tired at the wedding ceremonies, which would take place as soon as she arrived in Moscow.

There was the handsome carriage with a huge coachman and two footmen at her door, there was 5000 rubles—Nelidowa had never in her life seen so much money—there was the ring with a ruby, thick as a pigeon's egg, there was the confirmation of the Military Commander that all this was his work. Well, Nelidowa jumped into the carriage and did not travel in easy stages but in such haste, that the coachman often had to change his poor horses. Nelidowa didn't get tired at all. She was so excited that she did not feel the lack of sleep or food. She was in a trance.

She did not even lose this state of excitement when she saw the bridegroom. No poet could have made him into a desirable lover. He was in his middle fifties, short, brutal and bald, with a large belly, which protruded from underneath his hairy chest. Only when Nelidowa found herself with him in bed, did she realize the disgusting reality—but that must be told later on.

This was the reason why the young Princess plunged herself with such vigour into all and every kind of amusement and social debauchery. She had to make up for the past and she had to make the most of her bargain. Therefore, during the second season of her life in Moscow, she left no stone unturned if it meant any pleasure for herself. She treated her servants with reckless brutality, she became nervous, irritable and restless and was ceaselessly thinking of means to make everything as easy for herself as possible. She had decided that she did not want to try on her own clothes, but that a substitute should be found. That is how Katerina got her order to find and buy the duplicate of Madame.

Katerina had tried to fill this order for quite a while, that is, ever since Madame had got so many headaches trying on the last autumn styles. But so far Katerina had been unsuccessful. Not that the Princess had such an extraordinary figure. But those tramps, those peasant slave girls all had such miserable bodies; sturdy undercarriages, broad backs, large hips, terribly thick bottoms and legs. On the other hand, Nelidowa had very full, oval, pointed breasts, carried over an amazingly subtle waist. She had very well formed, straight legs and small, aristocratic hands and feet.

Nobody knew these differences better than the old housekeeper, because she herself had taken the measurements of Nelidowa's body. The 'little mother,' as her household serfs called her, had stood quite still as Katerina took her height, the measurements of her bust—above, over and below the full breast—of the waistline, the hips, the bottom, the thighs and the calves, the length of the arms and the legs. Nelidowa had stood quite still and had smiled, thinking it was the last time that she would have to do the trying-on herself.

Katerina had taken these measurements in her own way. She could not read or write, she could not handle the tape measure as those silly talking French clothiers did so skilfully. Therefore, she took ribbons of all colours, every time another colour for another measurement, and cut them exactly to the right length. She was able to remember without fail which colour represented, for example, the wrist or the ankle measurement, because this fat and

5

slightly grey and ignorant peasant woman had a better sense of recollection than any of the caste of learned and educated men. These coloured ribbons were then carefully sewn together so that they made a long string in the order in which Katerina was taking her measurements. In this way, a practical yardstick of Nelidowa's proportions was procured.

How often she had tried in vain! First she had gone around to the households of other Grandees and after a friendly chat with the Major Domo or with the head-housekeeper, she had looked the serf girls over, because it was always possible to buy a certain girl if no special reasons kept her in the household, such as the master liking her best as a bed companion. But not even among the ladies' maids and linen girls who were supposed to be of the finer kind, could she find any who came near her measurements. Then she had gone to the serf markets, which were held from time to time to make exchanges of serfs in the different houses of the aristocracy. After that, she had visited what one could call dealers; certain persons who had once been major domos and were liberated for one reason or another, and who made a scanty commission in buying and selling serfs, mostly young, good looking girls who were traded to the many whore houses which at that time started to flourish in Moscow, a fashion lately imported from Paris. In this way, Katerina had been hunting the whole winter, and while she found here and there a girl who came near the requirements, she had been told to bring a girl who would fit exactly. But how to get her?

This all was on Katerina's mind on that April afternoon (it must have been, approximately, in the year 1728) while she was on her way to a private dealer in the poor quarters of the North of Moscow. The sudden haste which crept up in her made her do something that was extraordinary for her. She hailed one of the droshkis which hung around a street corner, one of those dilapidated one-horse-carriages, which were not promising as to safe arrival at one's destination. The half drunken driver sullenly started with her, after she had made a hard bargain for the fare. Soon she found herself in a babbling conversation with the driver, who was her equal in being unable to keep his mouth shut, and who scratched his long hair when his ill-fed and tired horse stumbled over the rough cobblestones. Because it was not Katerina's way to keep anything to herself, the driver knew very soon that she was out to buy a serf girl for her Princess and mistress. Here he saw a chance for himself and told Katerina that a cousin of his, who had seen better days, was going to sell two of her girls, young and sturdy, and very obedient workers. But Katerina did not want to listen. She was determined to go to her destination and there they went. The driver was paid, and his remark that he would wait until his client got through with her business, received no answer.

Katerina was expected at the house of Ivan Drakeshkow, because she had sent him a message that she would look over his girls before they were offered at auction. She was greeted with dignity and almost reverence. A buyer with money is always welcome. Ivan Drakeshkow lived in a small, one storey house, surrounded by an untidy little garden, where some chickens were busy looking for prey after the rain. Ivan had bought the property when he was an ebony cutter, a successful craftsman in his line, and during this time, he had married the parlour maid of a Grandduchess, who had given the girl her liberty and a dowry. But Ivan had contracted an eye trouble which left him almost blind, and his wife, once good hearted and gay, had become a sour old witch who bossed him mercilessly. In fact it was she who started the trade in serfs and she earned just enough for food and fire-wood but never enough for a bottle of hard liquor, for which Ivan craved in vain. 'Who does not work shall not drink', was her motto, and she forced her good-for-nothing husband to wash the dishes.

Katerina was offered, with too much politeness, a huge and comfortable armchair. She was treated with tea from the ever-boiling samovar. She was drawn into long conversation about the Czar and her master. But she was in haste, uneasy, and wanted to see the girls. Madame Drakeshkow saw that the business had to be started right away.

'You see,' she said to Katerina, 'I will have for the auction more than twenty girls, but they are not all here yet. The later they come to me the less I have to feed the slobs. So if you don't find what you are looking for, just keep in touch with me and I am absolutely sure I can serve you. There is nobody who knows so well all the serf girls in town.' (She had only seven at present and did not expect to have more for her auction, which Katerina knew very well.)

She got up and went towards the bedroom next door to fetch the girls and presently came back with them, because they had been waiting to be called.

'Open up those curtains and get light in the room,' she called to her husband, who did obediently as told. After that he sat in a dark corner, looking at the wall. It was because of his eyes that the room was always kept in semi-darkness.

Katerina looked the seven girls over. They stood motionless in a row, in short Russian blouses and cheap, wide, woollen skirts; stockingless and in bare feet. Four of them Katerina dismissed right away, while Madame Drakeshkow praised eagerly the beauty and health of them all. The four, who were much too small or too tall, were very reluctantly sent away by Madame Drakeshkow, who was consoled by the demand of Katerina that the three remaining ones should take off their clothes. Buyers usually scrutinized the naked bodies minutely before purchase.

The stripping was quickly done. The blouses had to be unbuttoned, the skirts to be unhooked and the girls were nude. They now eyed Katerina, because she might become their future mistress, and although they discovered from her costume and bearing that she herself was only a serf, it was evident that she must be in an important position since she was delegated to buy new servants.

Katerina viewed the nude forms. Two of the girls were

8

impossible at a glance. One had very small, almost boyish breasts and of course the wide hips which were so common. The other one had such thick thighs and so broad a bottom, that she might already have had a couple of children. Katerina disregarded them entirely and though they stayed in the room, it was only because it had been forgotten to send them away. Katerina now motioned the last girl nearer to the window and took out, to the amazement of Madame Drakeshkow, the above mentioned multicoloured ribbons. With some misgivings she started with the height, (which was correct) came to the bust, where more than the thickness of two fingers was missing and gave it up when the hips proved more than a hand's breadth too large. With a sigh, she put her ribbon back in her sack and moved without speaking to the exit-door. She paid no attention to the rain of words by the utterly bewildered Madame Drakeshkow, who had not under-stood what she had been about. To measure a servant girl! Who had ever heard of such folly? But Katerina was already on the street with the look of a beaten dog in her eyes, undecided what to do next.

The droshki driver, warmed meanwhile by a drink from a nearby public house, saluted her cheerfully and coaxed her to hire him again. He hoped that her eminence had completed her mission perfectly and that he could drive her home in roaring speed. Katerina let him know that she had been unsuccessful and that by the name of her personal Saint, she would have to give up. Then the befuddled driver remembered that she wanted to buy some girls, and anew praised the goods which his cousin wanted to dispose of. He'd drive her over quickly and—

Katerina looked at the sun. It was still early. One unsuccessful try more or less did not matter and she climbed back into the carriage, which answered with a sigh, bending to her weight.

We soon see Katerina heavily breathing while climbing up a creaking and steep staircase to the cousin's attic. It turned out that this cousin, a thin spinster of about fifty years, was handling an embroidery business on a small scale; that she had two girls working for her; and that she wanted to give up her enterprise and leave Moscow in order to stay with relatives in the South. Lacking money for the long trip, the sale of the two girls should provide the means. Katerina was led into the adjoining room, a large, very light attic room, bare of any furniture except a work table crowded with materials of all kinds.

On a bench before this table, bent over their work, sat two girls. The cousin commanded them to rise and it was then that Katerina uttered a cry of amazement. One of the girls was an exact duplicate of her Princess; at least her face and features were so perfectly like those of her mistress that Katerina first feared a spook might have tricked her. Still, the face did not matter at all. It was only the right contours of the body which were sought. The height was right, the form seemed so, and Katerina hastily demanded that this dark haired girl with the shining blue eyes be stripped. The other girl was a short, flat nosed, sturdy creature and Katerina disregarded her. Not so the cousin. She made it quite clear that she would not sell one girl alone; it must be both or neither. Katerina mumbled that all that could be arranged, just let her see the dark one.

The girls, who had no previous knowledge that their Madame wanted to get rid of them, flushed slightly, looked at each other and at the cousin, and stood sheepishly. The cousin slapped the dark girl and demanded to know whether she had become deaf and when she wanted to start to take her clothes off. With excited fingers, the buttons of the blouse opened; then came a bodice of common linen, strapped and fastened with many ribbons, and from underneath a rough chemise stood out two full and hard breasts with deep red nipples.

Katerina, the never-smiling, grinned. It was the kind of bust she was looking for. The wide skirt of flowered and cheap material fell to the floor and a pair of wide trousers, reaching to the ankles, came to view. A bush of thick black hair protruded through the open slit of the drawers, which was there for the sake of commodity. (The women of that time attended to their natural functions through the gap

10

of their trousers, which they opened up while sitting down for the necessity.)

Soon shirt and drawers were also removed and Katerina eyed her find with growing satisfaction. She went around and around the nude girl. The waistline was perfect; the legs full and female but subtle and the flesh of the arse seemed to be even softer than that of her mistress. To find out, she came close to the girl and felt her body. She was content. This was not the usual peasant type. This was not a tough and common brat. This girl had the form of an aristocrat, a form which must be like that of her 'little mother.'

Katerina remembered her measurements, took out her ribbons and began her comparisons. Well, the height was almost perfect, a little too tall, but she could tolerate that small difference. The length of the back, the breasts, the waistline, the thickness of the thighs were right or what one might call right. Even the wrists and the ankles fitted. It turned out that the length of the legs, measured from the slit to the floor, was a trifle too long, but Katerina had already resolved that this girl was to be bought.

When the last measurement was taken and Katerina, kneeling on the floor, had touched the pussy, the girl had drawn slightly and irritatedly back. For the rest, she had behaved quietly and with that absence of shamefulness or shyness characteristic of other serf girls. These girls did not know of the existence of anything like shame. From early youth on their bodies were at the disposal of their masters and their secret parts were no more theirs than their hands or faces.

The bargaining started. Katerina wanted to buy only the dark girl and she did not want to pay more than 50 rubles; the blonde imp was not wanted; her master owned 100,000 souls and did not need any more. The cousin shrieked that then he did not need to buy the dark girl either. While Katerina zealously defended the money of her master, the blonde girl leaned against the table and the nude dark one stood motionless with hanging arms in the middle of the room, as if she had nothing to do with the affair. The driver here and there interjected an appeasing word from the door, where he loitered as a witness who is waiting for a handsome commission. The cousin was thin and hard. Katerina was eager to buy and after a battle, the old housekeeper's hand went into the bodice which covered her enormous bosom and brought to light an ugly leather purse, from which she paid the cousin 90 rubles in glittering gold. She had got the price down from the demanded hundred, but she had to take both girls.

No, she was not sending a carriage for them. She was going to take both with her. She was afraid she might lose her precious discovery. They would start immediately. The girls had nothing to pack. They had no belongings except some woollen kerchiefs and the like, which were quickly made into a bundle. After the dark girl was hurriedly dressed again, Katerina took a quick leave with her purchase, though not without assuring the cousin anew that the price paid had been outrageous. The cousin made the sign of the cross over her former serfs. They in turn, automatically and without feeling, kissed the hem of her dress and soon the three women sat in the carriage. The driver was paid a little distance from Sokolow's house and received what he demanded. It is quite sure that with this money and the commission from his cousin, he was senselessly drunk for several days.

Starting towards the palace, Katerina asked the dark girl what her name was. 'Grushenka,' answered the girl, readily. That was the first word she spoke after she had become one of the uncounted souls of Prince Alexey Sokolow. She did not know then the name of her new master.

CHAPTER II.

It must be remembered that our story takes place shortly after the death of Peter the Great and that the revolutionary changes he had made during his violent dictatorship came at this time to their first blossom. Peter the Great had done away with the seclusion of women who had lived before then in the oriental life of the harem. He had forced them into society, where they were at first so awkward that he got them drunk in order to loosen them up. He had lifted the Bojars, the aristocratic caste, to an elevated position by forcing the working class into unheard of servitude and submission. He had, by the most cruel tortures, in which he participated personally, built up a social order in which might was God and the serf a slave. He had forced Western culture upon his Bojars and one of his orders had been that they should build themselves great castles and houses.

Alexey Sokolow was only a score of years the junior of this great ruler. While eager to take all the advantages which were offered to his class, he had enough cunning to see that it was wiser to stay away from the inner court circle, where the greatest generals or officials were uncertain when they would find themselves on the rack or the wheel and eventually beheaded. Sokolow had therefore established his city life in Moscow instead of St. Petersburg and here in Moscow he had erected the magnificent palace which can be seen to this day.

Katerina dismissed the droshki a few blocks away, so as not to be seen by other servants riding in a hired carriage, and led the two bewildered serf girls to the huge arch of the main entrance guarded by two soldiers with muskets, high tin helmets and high boots. They paid no attention to the three women who quickly entered the archway and were admitted to the inner courtyard.

Flowers, lampoons, grass, even bushes covered the tremendous square of the inner court. Tables, chairs and benches stood about in great disorder. This courtyard was normally a barren place of cobblestones, but the Princess had given an entertainment the night before for which the flowers and grass had been raised in hothouses in the country.

Katerina gave her wards no time to look or to think. She hurried them through the court and down a stone staircase to the basement, which consisted of endless halls and rooms and kitchens. Here Katerina left the blonde girl with a woman who seemed to be an overseer of this underground labyrinth. She then took Grushenka by the hand and marched on with her. This time she led her up a small and winding wooden staircase, which ended at the second floor. Thick Turkish carpets covered the light hallway and Grushenka soon saw a room which she was going to know very thoroughly afterwards. It was the try-on room of the Princess, fitted with a big oak table in the middle of the room and huge chestnut closets and presses along the walls between which mirrors of all kinds and dimensions were installed.

On a curt order from Katerina the girl took all her clothes off, and entirely nude, was dragged by the old housekeeper through other rooms, which were magnificently adorned with silks and brocades. Through the half open door of her mistress's boudoir. Katerina led the substitute of Madame, in her excitement not waiting for permission to enter.

The Princess was sitting before a mirror at her toilet table. Boris, the coiffeur, was busy curling her long dark brown hair. A young serf girl, sobbing apparently from a recent thrashing, knelt on the floor and put rouge on her mistress's toe-nails. In the corner, near a window, sat 'Fräulein,' an elderly spinster who had been a German governess in different houses of the great, and who was now reading aloud in a dry and monotonous voice some French poetry. The Princess listened with slight understanding or interest. The French poet had worked into his fable all kinds of persons from the Greek and Latin mythology, which meant nothing to the capricious listener. But when he described how the enormous shaft of Mars was pushed into the grotto of Venus, that called for noticeable attention.

In her mirror Princess Nelidowa had seen Katerina appearing with Grushenka and waved angrily not to be disturbed. So Grushenka had an opportunity to study the group just described. The Princess wore only a short batiste chemise which left her more or less uncovered. She did not mind that Boris, clad in the formal house uniform of the Sokolows with a long pig-tail at his back, could see her nudity, because he was only a serf. He had been sent to Dresden some years ago to learn the art of hairdressing with a very famous master in the Saxonian capital. Sokolow had intended to rent him out to one of the ladies' hairdressing parlours recently opened in Moscow, but the Princess had taken the clever fellow into her private service. He was responsible for her many tufts and locks worn in the daytime and for her powdered wigs decorated with precious stones which went with the evening gowns.

When the reading of the poem had ceased, Katerina could restrain herself no longer. 'I have her! I have her!' she cried and dragged Grushenka closer to the Princess. 'I found a substitute who fits perfectly and she is ours now!'

'I know you could have found her sooner,' said Nelidowa, maliciously. 'But you'll be forgiven since you dug her up at last. Now show me, does she really have the measurements or are you lying to me?' She rose hastily from her stool, so that poor Boris was in danger of burning her with his hot irons.

'She really and truly fits,' answered Katerina. 'Here, I'll show you,' and took out the multicoloured ribbons to prove the fact. But Nelidowa was not interested in that. With sharp eyes she scrutinized Grushenka's body and she was not dissatisfied.

'So! That is how I look. A full pair of good breasts, aren't they? But mine are better!'—and taking out without concern her own breasts from her thin shirt and holding them close to Grushenka's she started a minute comparison—'Mine are oval and that is rare, but this slob's are round. Look at her

15

nipples! How big and common!'—and she tickled with her own nipples those of the girl.

Now it is true, there was a slight difference, but hardly noticeable. Nelidowa then took hold of Grushenka's waist with both hands and did not handle her too tenderly.

'I always said,' the mistress continued, 'That I have an excellent waist-line and here one can see it. Among all the court ladies, not one can compare with me.'

That it was not her own waist-line she admired but that of her new slave girl did not come to her mind. She proceeded to the thighs which she pinched, surprised by Grushenka's very soft flesh. 'My legs,' she commented, displaying now her own thighs and squeezing them a bit, 'are sturdier than those of this little bitch, but we'll take the softness out of her.' With mock laughter she commanded Grushenka to turn around.

Nelidowa as well as Grushenka had a remarkably well modelled back; round female shoulders, soft and full lines down to the bottom, small and well rounded hips. Only Grushenka's buttocks were too small, almost boyish and went too evenly and straight to the thighs. Her legs and feet were normal and straight and could have been used by artists as models.

'Now!' laughed the Princess. 'This is the first time that I see my own back and truly I like it. Isn't it fine that this tramp should have just my back. Next time my father confessor demands that I inflict some lashes on my own poor back I can take hers as my substitute and I can be generous with the number of blows I give myself.' To demonstrate this splendid idea, she gave a goodly pinch to Grushenka's flesh below the right shoulder blade. Grushenka twisted her mouth a bit but stood motionless and without a cry. She was confused by what was happening and would have stood a greater shock without moving.

The witnesses of this scene, especially Katerina, were astonished by the similarity between these two women as they stood close together. It was astounding to see that not only the figures, but the features and faces of both were so much alike that one could have sworn they were twin sisters.

Nature sometimes plays tricks of that kind. Grushenka was younger, she had a whiter skin; she blushed at present in her excitement and looked fresher. Also her flesh was softer and a bit more female than that of Nelidowa and she had a timid bearing and was not so self-contained as the Princess. Otherwise, they were strangely alike, though no one would have dared to tell this to the Princess.

'I am pleased with you, and I'll present you with my new prayer book with the pictures of the Saints in it which you admired the other day. It's yours. Go and get it.' Katerina with a deep curtsy kissed her mistress's hand, overjoyed that she had at last satisfied her. She was taking the girl out of the room when she was stopped by a last word of her mistress, who watched the nude form depart.

'By the way, Katerina, have all the hair under her arms and on her dirty cunt removed so that she doesn't infect my garments. And have her spotlessly washed and powdered. You know how filthy these pigs are.' Katerina assured her she would have the girl taken care of.

Katerina had Grushenka take her clothes over her arm and went with her again to the basement. She knew that both girls had to be taken in as new serfs and she took care of the requirements usual on such occasions in her efficient way.

Grushenka and the other girl sat a few minutes later before a huge cleanly washed table. Soon plates with food, brought quickly by other serf girls, piled up before them. A new serf was always fed to the utmost by the new master and the girls were hardly able to do justice to the resources of the kitchen of Prince Sokolow. Their former diet as supplied by the stingy cousin had consisted of coarse bread, onions and rice and many of the dishes which now stood before them were utterly unknown to them. They ate all they could but had to give up when a big apple pudding proved too much for their filled stomachs.

Grushenka had been sitting nude through the meal. When they had eaten, the blonde girl was asked to take her clothes off. They were then requested by the woman in charge of the basement to throw their clothes into the big stove of the kitchen, where they soon burned away. A great

17

master would not allow a servant to wear clothes another master had previously given him and also it was well known that clothes often brought the germs of disease into a house. Pest and smallpox were flourishing and no precaution against these scourges of the time could be omitted. After this the girls were brought over to the servants' bath, where a few bath-girls waited for them. They were soaped all over with a stinging soap and afterwards put in two wooden tubs with very hot water so that their skin became red as boiled lobsters. They were then pushed into the steam room which was in charge of a one armed invalid, a former soldier and bodyguard of the Prince. He did not look at the girls. He merely coughed and muttered vile and disgruntled words, because his body and mind were unbalanced.

Grushenka sat in the large, bare room with its wet brick walls and steaming boilers and began for the first time to give herself an accounting of the last few hours. From the poor rooms of the morose and thin cousin, she had been brought to the fairy palace of a Prince. For what, she could not understand. And while she wiped away the pearls of water which collected on her bust and belly, she whispered to her companion, 'What do they want of me? What do you think they want?' But the blonde one whispered back that it would be ten thousand times better than before and that Prince Sokolow—they had learned the name from the girls who had previously served them—had so many thousands of serfs that if they managed rightly, they certainly would have the time of their lives. So far it was too good for words: a dinner of abundance, a real bath as was given only to fine people; even a steam-room for the servants! Who would have dreamt of that?

Presently they were called out of the steam-room, their skin loosened by the heat, and were given a very cold washing with clean water which was poured on them from buckets. They shivered and screamed trying to avoid the gushes but it was quickly over. Then they were rubbed with thick towels and dried thoroughly.

Katerina now took hold of them again to bring them to their quarters. The male servants lived in the stables or over the stables. The women had their quarters in the loft of the main house which was under the supervision of an elderly serf woman. Breathing heavily, Katerina led the way up the back stairs, scolding herself inwardly for going so seldom to the loft. (She herself had a chamber in the basement.) Her old knees resented the many hundred steps.

The upper floor of the palace contained many rooms and large halls in some of which were rows of wooden beds and board closets for clothing and linen. The woman in charge rose out of a half slumber to meet Katerina's unexpected visit and showed the girls to two unoccupied beds at the end of one of the halls. She left upon Katerina's command to fetch some linen and garments for the newcomers and Katerina, catching her breath again, turned to the girls.

'I did not look you over before buying you,' she said to the blonde and stocky girl. 'It was my duty, but I hope you are clean and will not bring sickness to the house. Let me look you over now.' The blonde girl grinned, knowing she was healthy as a bear and that her brown skin did not easily take infection. Katerina started her inspection in a matter of fact way. She opened the girl's mouth and looked over the teeth, which were sharp as those of an animal. She fingered the small breasts. (The girl was not more than seventeen years old.) She looked over the flesh of the belly, the legs, the back, under the arms and finally had the girl lie down over the bed and with her legs spread open. She opened the lips of the cunt and felt with one finger for the virgin membrane which was still in place. Katerina understood these things. She had helped many women in child bed and had acted as midwife when any of the women of the household gave birth. She did not disregard the arse hole, which might indicate a sickness of the stomach—but the girl was in good shape and underwent these operations with the stubborn submissiveness of the Russian serf.

Katerina then addressed the girls with a little speech as was usual on such occasions. She pointed out that as they had eaten today, so would they continue to eat, that they would be clothed and housed in splendid manner and that they were to be proud to be the servants of the noble Prince

19

Sokolow. On the other hand they were required to be extremely obedient and industrious and to do their best for their new master. If they failed in that, they would be punished heavily and so it would be to their own good to submit to rules and orders.

To make this clear to them, and to inaugurate them into the household, she would now give them a light and friendly whipping, hoping she would never again have the necessity to do so. She then ordered Grushenka, to whom this address was mostly delivered, to lie on the bed in order to receive the strokes. Meanwhile the woman had come back with blankets and linen and hearing Katerina's words, brought from the middle of the hall, two buckets in which fresh switches were kept in salt water.

Grushenka laid down on the bed on her stomach and buried her head in her hands. Often as she had been submitted to bodily chastisement, she could not endure it. She trembled, and kept her legs close together in nervous tension. But that was not to Katerina's liking, who saw it as an act of revolt. Roughly she pulled apart the girls legs, shouting at her to loosen up the muscles and to be still or she would give her the much more painful leather whip.

"Didn't you hear what the Princess said?' she added. 'We'll take the softness out of you, you yellow dog,' and she started to prepare the fine bottom for the punishment by squeezing hard the full flesh, even pulling the hair of the Mount of Venus, which protruded between the legs. Katerina now had evil eyes, her mouth was tightly shut and the nostrils of her nose moved greedily. Such a little imp of a serf, making a fuss because she was to get the switch! Grushenka groaned and tried to stop quivering, but she was so frightened she could hardly control herself. Katerina took a switch from the servant woman and ordered the blonde girl who watched the proceedings without emotion, to count aloud to twenty-five.

The first blow went over the right side of the bottom and it was a heavy stroke, because Katerina was angry and was a muscular peasant woman. Grushenka cried out and bent her body up as if she wanted to rise but put herself again in position. The second blow and the next few went over the same thigh, where a crimson pattern appeared in sharp contrast to the whiteness of the rest of the body. Katerina proceeded to the other thigh which was next to her, and laid blow after blow with great firmness on the skin.

Grushenka screamed and shook her body, but she did not move away and always got back into position. She had received almost twenty-five blows. Katerina had several times changed the switches which broke into pieces. When Katerina applied the last strokes to the insides of the legs which had not been hit before, it was too much for Grushenka. She rolled over to the wall and held both hands to her bottom pleading for mercy and protesting she could not stand it. But Katerina was not willing to give way to a young and obstinate serf girl. Therefore, with an energy and brutality which one would not have suspected in this fat and greyish housekeeper, she forced Grushenka to the middle of the bed, laying her on her back with her arms folded under her head and spread the girls legs open with rude force. 'If your arse can't stand it,' she shouted at the frightened girl, 'then your front can have it and don't dare to move, because if you do, I'll have some stable men put you on the rack and give you the cow-hide and we'll see how you'll like that.'

She began with fierce strokes to whip the inside and the front of the thighs. Grushenka was so thoroughly paralysed and frightened that she did not dare to close her legs or to protect herself with her hands, although she moved instinctively to do so. She received about ten strokes in this way and although Katerina avoided striking the open cunt, for Grushenka it was an agony which seemed endless.

Finally it was over. Katerina's eyes remained fixed on the growth of hair around the cunt and on the slit itself. She had forgotten to find out whether this girl was virgin or not and she stooped without ceremony to make the examination. As soon as she touched the lips of the pussy, Grushenka became convulsive, partly because she expected more painful punishment, partly because she was sensitive at that spot. Katerina pushed her down and shoved her finger into the hole and found the resistance of the membrane. (The cousin

21

must have had her girls under close observation, because these hussies usually liked nothing better than to fuck.)

Grushenka was still a virgin and as far as Katerina was concerned, she should remain so. She had forgotten her own youth and the thrill she used to get out of a good poke, and kept her girls under very strict watch. She was through with Grushenka now and ordered her to get up and looked with disdain at the crying, twitching face. What a soft girl, who could not stand such a little punishment!

Without much enthusiasm, she turned to the blonde creature. She ordered her to lie on her back and to move her legs up so that her feet touched her shoulders. The blonde did so without hesitation. She had a thick skin and a whipping more or less did not matter much in her young life. Katerina felt the flesh of the firm arse which was in this position put conveniently at her disposal. She was hardly able to squeeze the bottom because the flesh was so hard that it did not move under her fingers. She gave the girl some twenty strokes, not so severe as those she had given Grushenka, and the blonde one counted the strokes herself in a subdued but clear voice. It was one of those quick and unexciting beatings which mean nothing because the beating party is not much concerned with the job and the receiving party is more annoyed than hurt. When it was over the blonde one rubbed her arse and that was all.

Katerina had both girls kiss the end of the switch which she held in her hands, then ordered them to go to bed and stay there until they were called the next day to their respective duties. The blonde was to join the sewing crew, because she was handy with the needle after her education by the cousin, and Katerina herself would take care of Grushenka.

Both girls crept dully between the sheets, Grushenka sobbing, and the other one quite content.

'What do they want of me?' sobbed Grushenka. 'What can they want? ...' until she fell asleep.

CHAPTER III.

The next morning, quite early, Grushenka who had slept soundly in a bed that seemed to her the best she had ever had, was awakened by noisy shouting. With wondering eyes she looked about her. A hundred girls and women seemed to enliven the big loft, yawning, shouting, babbling and laughing in a confusion of washing and teasing and dressing and admonishments to hurry up. Actually, there were only sixty-three servant girls housed here, ranging in age from fifteen to about thirty-five. Younger and older women were not kept in the city palace.

The girls put on all kinds of dresses, according to their duties; the kitchen maids dark woollen garments; the linen and silver maids, a white uniform-like costume; the sewing squad, flowery cashmeres. The personal chamber and bedmaids of the Princess, about eight or ten, and the special favourites of the Prince, slept near the apartments of their masters. Some privileged elderly women and cooks had quarters in the basement.

Soon they were all sitting on long benches in a big hall near the kitchen in the basement and steaming soups and white bread were devoured in great quantities. Katerina always saw to it that the servants got plenty to eat. Not that she was concerned with their likes and desires. She simply wanted to keep them content and healthy, to enable them to perform their duties to the last ounce. Katerina was quite a fanatic on this point and any shirker could be sure of the whip, if not of a harder punishment.

After breakfast, Grushenka received the short order to go to the bathroom. She could not imagine why. She never before had been allowed more than one bath in a month; bathing was expensive because it meant fire-wood. Yet, now she was bathed and scrubbed thoroughly. Furthermore, the bath-girls were told to clean her up every day right after the breakfast and to see to it that she was spotless or else they would be sorry. The bath-girls took no chances and they scrubbed and rubbed and cleaned her everywhere and anywhere. Grushenka then was told to take her clothes over her arm and to wait in the try-on room for Katerina. There she sat now, on an oaken trunk, full of precious silks and embroideries, shivering after the bath, her clothes clutched to her body. Many maids passed through the room, walking here and there, sometimes giving her a friendly nod, mostly not taking notice of her.

Presently Katerina appeared and seeing Grushenka, she went to a closet and got a box of powder and a big powder-puff. She proceeded to teach her how to powder her whole body, omitting no part. Then she suddenly remembered the shaving business. She sent for Boris, who was soon there with his outfit of razors and soap. 'You heard what her Highness said, yesterday,' she addressed the barber. 'Shave cleanly her hair under the arms and between the legs. But don't cut her. We paid a big price for the bitch.'

Boris made Grushenka hold both her arms straight up and soaped and shaved her under the arms, quite cleverly and quickly. He then glanced over to see if Katerina was still there. He had never before shaved a girl's cunt and wanted to have some fun with it. But Katerina stood solidly there, leaning on an oaken stick and she looked sternly at Boris, who quickly avoided her eyes.

Grushenka was now laid on a table with her legs apart. Katerina saw that the marks of the switch were clearly visible in red-violet welts. 'She has a softer skin than all of them,' thought the old housekeeper, but not with pity, rather with a resolution that she would thrash the girl oftener in order to get her used to it.

Grushenka was trembling nervously as Boris, with his scissors, cut the long curls from her Mount of Venus and below. He then soaped her with his brush, not sparing the lips of the cunt, and finally expanded the skin with two fingers on his left hand. There followed the soft grating of

24

the knife, that cut the hair closely to the white flesh. He started to put his fingers between the lips of the slit as if to extend the skin better, but Katerina tapped sharply with her stick and he thought better of it. A wet towel was now applied and the job was done.

Open lay Grushenka's cunt. The fine red lips were slightly apart. Rather long lips with the entrance hole settled down quite low, right in the neighbourhood of the arse hole, which was small and well contracted. Boris, now in possession of a throbbing erection, was mad to make use of this delectable shaven pussy. He even would have liked to suck it a bit, to tickle and taste its naked contours with his tongue. But Katerina sent him scooting and he was forced to find solace with less alluring material. There were many girls about who were enamoured of his sturdy prick and he quickly managed to find a dark corner and a soft hole in which to get rid of his load.

Katerina called out to the sewing rooms next door that a couple of dressing girls should come in. She now had Grushenka dressed up in one of the Princess's outfits to see whether she would really do as a model for the new summer wardrobe. Long silk stockings were applied, a chemise with golden threads was put on her. Long trousers, fitted and closed with ribbons on the ankles, came next. A crimson bodice without stays was tied on. (Stays were worn in Western Europe at that time, but not in Russia, where the elegant women liked to show their breasts with the nipples sticking out above their dresses.) A tunic, which took the place of the skirt and blouse, then was hooked and buttoned and over this fell a long loose cloak, leaving the arms underneath bare. During this procedure all the girls of the tailoring and sewing departments had left their work and watched eagerly. When Grushenka was ready and was told to walk up and down the large room, turning and displaying the costume and herself, the watchers clapped their hands and stamped their feet. 'That is our Princess!' they cried, 'Just like her! Can you imagine?' Katerina heard this outburst with satisfaction. Yes, she had found the clothes-horse for her mistress.

Grushenka was instructed that she was to be used from now on as the fitting model for her Highness. Then and there started for Grushenka a long period of waiting and dreaming, dreaming and waiting until some dress-maker would come around and fit some garments on her, turning her around, trying on, admiring his own craftsmanship, or cursing the sewing girls who had done a bad job. These try-ons were at first very displeasing to Grushenka, because all these workers, men and women, some of them serfs, some of them free people, who called themselves artists, touched her body all over and took many liberties with her. This was all the more so because she was such a perfect counterfeit of her Madame, before whom these men crawled on their bellies.

It was thus fine fun for them to paw her breasts, to pinch her nipples and to play around quite abundantly with her pussy. This last Grushenka hated especially and she tried to shove them away, only to be stuck painfully with a needle in the buttocks or in the breast. So she got used to it, especially when she found that when she resisted she was plagued much more, but if she kept still, the men were not so insistent. It usually went along this way: A little tailor's helper, who had the order to try something on her, would put his finger in her cunt and would say, 'Fine morning, your Highness. How did you like the prick of the Prince last night?' and laughing at his own joke, would begin his work.

Months went by this way, first in the palace in Moscow, then at one of the great estates in the country; months of dreaming and waiting. Of course, Grushenka, meanwhile, got well acquainted with the great household. She listened to the gossip about the brutal and drunken Prince, whom the Princess hated, but played up to; of the young lover the Princess had taken; of the way she had her bedmaids make love to her to satisfy her everlasting cravings. But Grushenka heard these tales without taking notice and nobody seemed to take much notice of her. It was hard to say of what she was thinking, maybe of the clouds which passed along or of a bird in the big tree ouside the window.

Then came the day which changed her whole life. The Princess had been out to a party and it had turned out badly.

Even her lover had neglected her, had flirted openly with a rival. The Princess had drunk too much, had had an argument with another lady and her husband, the Prince, furious with such misbehaviour had slapped her face violently while driving her home. Nelidowa was wild. She accused everybody but herself. She let the whip fly freely on the backs of the girls who undressed her and still was not able to ease her rage. When she saw her brocade gown with the silver stripes lying on the floor, she suddenly remembered that Grushenka had modelled it for her approval that same afternoon. In her crazed state, she imagined that this gown and thus the girl who had displayed it, were responsible for her misadventures.

It was two o'clock at night and Grushenka was fast asleep, when she was dragged naked from her bed. Drunk with sleepiness and knowing of no fault she had committed, the girl was taken before her mistress. The Princess, now in bed, accused her in the vilest terms of having induced her to wear an unbecoming dress and ordered one of her chamber maids to lash Grushenka over her bare back with the leather whip which lay always ready for this purpose on the toilet table. Another maid stepped in front of Grushenka, turning her back toward her, took the arms of the frightened girl over her shoulders and bent forward so that Grushenka lost her foothold on the floor and lay helplessly on the back of the chamber maid.

The whipping started at once. The strokes cut whistling through the air. The shoulders, the back, the behind were hit and hit by a rain of blows. Grushenka did not know that the whipping girl applied the punishment with great craftmanship, cracking the whip loudly but taking care that the lash cut the flesh as little as possible, for this girl was angry at her Madame and sorry for the innocent victim. In spite of this fact, Grushenka underwent awful pain and screamed and kicked her legs as well as she could. The Princess lay in her bed, her teeth bared in rage, her fingers with their long nails held in the form of claws as if she wanted to scratch the flesh off the girl's bones.

Although not told so, the whipping girl finally ceased

beating as if she were exhausted from swinging the lash and Nelidowa did not command her to go on because she felt suddenly sick from the liquor she had drunk. Grushenka was now lowered to the floor and putting both her hands to her aching arse she walked straddle legged from the room. At this moment the eyes of the Princess fixed on Grushenka's slit, which having been shaven as usual was entirely open to sight. The Princess stared hard at this slit because it was formed differently than her own and while the girl was supposed to have a body similar to hers, the cunt certainly was an exception.

Nelidowa did not say a word about this dissimilarity, but she kept the thought in her mind. There had been an instance, when something seemingly had been wrong with her own pussy and she could not make out what it was.

There happened to be in Moscow at that time a Spaniard, an adventurer who lived by his wits, a chevalier no doubt, but a shady character and fortune seeker. He was permitted to mix in society because he represented the higher and so much admired Western culture. Also because he could tell such elegantly slippery stories and all kinds of gossip from the bed-chambers of the well known gentlemen and ladies in Paris, London and Vienna. This lady-charmer, with his glittering eyes and short black moustache (he had no long beard as the good Russians wore), had the reputation of kissing a lady's cunt, an act which was unthinkable to a Russian Nobleman and a fashion which had been brought lately from Italy to Paris, so it was said. Nelidowa had made up her mind to capture this gentleman for that very purpose. She had managed to sit next to him at the gambling table one evening and had stacked a pile of gold rubles on his side. These she then tipped over with her elbow in his direction. The gold which she showered towards him she did not reclaim.

Of course, the gentleman made use of this opportunity and later in the night walked with her through the park, where they sat down on a bench. His words had flown in a stream of romance and he had admired her beautiful feet which aroused his passion to such a degree that he just had to

28

kiss them. He had started with the feet and had gone tenderly up the calves and landed on the thighs, which he kissed fervently. Nelidowa, apparently overcome by his ardour, had bent back, opening ever so lightly and with apprehension her well-shaped legs so that the slit in her trousers permitted any intrusion which might be wanted. The chevalier had then spread open this slit with his aristocratic fingers, pressed many kisses on the small part of the belly and approached by degrees the pussy. He had furthermore sucked with his lips the flesh close to the very entrance. Then suddenly, he had stopped. He pressed a quick kiss on the slit and went up abruptly, without doing the very thing for which she had prepared so carefully.

That evening when she came home Nelidowa had investigated before a mirror to learn what was wrong with her grotto. Yes, the lips of her cunt were thick and flappy and left the entrance which they were supposed to close, quite open. But had not all married women such cunts and what was the matter with hers? At any rate that night Nelidowa had one of her bed girls suck her cunt for hours and when the girl got tired and did not rub the tickler with her tongue strongly and quickly enough, her mistress promised her the whip if she did not suck more effectively.

How was it that Grushenka had a nicer cunt than she herself? How was it that her own pussy was not good enough for this scoundrel and cheat of a Spanish adventurer? One afternoon, when Nelidowa lay idly on her couch, she made up her mind to find out and forthwith sent for Grushenka. She made the girl take her clothes off and was glad to see the blue and red stripes which the whip had left, especially on one side of the body where the end of the strap had cut the flesh. She asked Grushenka to come very close to her, straddle legged, so that she could inspect the girl's pussy. Of course the slit was very finely made; the Princess had to tell herself that in spite of the anger she felt. The lips were thin and rosy and cut the oval of the Venus hill in an even curve which did not stick out and puff up like her own. She made Grushenka hold the cunt open with her fingers. The slit was shallow and of a bright red and the vagina had its opening near a small hole on the lowest part of the body between the legs. With her eyes on the girl's spot, but without fingering her, Nelidowa started to question her.

'When were you fucked last?' she began. Grushenka hardly understood the meaning of the question. But the Princess insisted, 'How long ago is it, since you were poked by a prick?' Now Grushenka knew what was meant and answered quite firmly, 'No man has ever touched me, your Highness. I am a virgin.' 'Oh!' thought the Princess, 'Of course when I was still with the nuns my pussy was probably like hers, but since that old bastard (by which she meant of course the Prince) every so often puts his damned machine in my hole . . .' But aloud she said with laughter, 'I'll fix you up my child and that right now. Never fucked! Still a pimply virgin, eh? You lie down here now and we'll soon attend to you.'

She got up from the couch with some spirit. She enjoyed this splendid idea. It would pass the time piquantly. Who to get for the job? Oh, yes, there was her riding groom, that broad-shouldered fellow with the big bush of tousled hair. His blondness would make a good match for Grushenka's deep black hair. Nelidowa had looked sometimes with longing at Ivan (she had a habit of calling all male servants Ivan) and had more than once glanced over his muscular arms and legs and rested her eyes on his trousers. She would have tried him herself, but she had no desire for the brand of brutal male love which her husband supplied. However, this was just the right man to rape that stupid lump on the couch.

Ivan had been loading hay. When he came in, in linen trousers and an open shirt, hay was still clinging to his hair and clothes and he brought with him the smell of the stable. Meanwhile the five or six chambermaids who were always around their mistress, had not been idle. They enjoyed in advance, like Madame, the spectacle which was coming. They had put a pillow under Grushenka's bottom, with much giggling they had smeared some salve in her gap, they had put their fingers in her hole, and pitied her in mock tones, that she was going to be torn. Grushenka lay very still, her hands clasped to her face, uneasy and wondering. Perhaps she had dreamt during the past months of the lover to whom she wanted to give herself. Perhaps she had made him a romantic hero, some man from the moon. Yet here she lay waiting to be ravished by a stable boy.

'Ivan,' said the Princess, 'I have called you because this poor girl complained to me that no man ever made love to her and that her virginity is itching her terribly. I chose you to give her the fuck of her life. Go on my boy and make a poor longing virgin happy. Get your tool out and screw the bitch.'

Ivan looked bewildered from his mistress to the nude form on the couch and again from one to the other. He fingered his hands before his body as though he were holding a cap and turning it uneasily around. He did not move. Was it a trap or was it serious? The Princess was becoming impatient.

'Get your trousers down and fuck! Don't you hear?' she shouted at him.

Ivan mechanically opened up his trousers. They fell to his feet and he pulled his shirt up over his navel. The eyes of all the girls, except Grushenka's, stared at his big dark brown balls and an equally dark brown, big tool which hung its head listlessly and unfit for work.

'Now go over and kiss your bride,' continued the mistress, leaning on the toilet table and rubbing her own cunt with the palm of her hand, being a bit excited. Slowly, Ivan moved to the couch, then with a determination to go ahead, he took Grushenka's hands from her face, bent over her and kissed her on the mouth. The chamber maids applauded. But Grushenka lay so lifeless that Ivan lost pluck again. He fidgeted, looked at the naked girl and at the others and did nothing more. His prick was still in its flabby condition. It was again the Princess who had to bring the proceedings to life.

'Lay on top of her, you stupid ass!' she cried. 'And you,' pointing to one of her girls, 'You, give that prick of his a good finger feeling or suck him prettily so that he gets stiff, the big swine.'

As ordered, so was it done. Ivan, hindered in his movements by the trousers around his ankles, laid himself on top of Grushenka and a bed maid, obeying the order she had received, caressed his tool with apt fingers. Another girl, quite voluntarily attracted by his firm bare arse, started to squeeze it a little and playfully inserted a finger in his arse hole. Ivan was a tough and sturdy stableman, so no wonder that his prick began to swell and grow under such treatment. And suddenly he began to enjoy the job to which he had been assigned.

His prick became a stiff lance. His muscular behind started uneasy and nervous movements and he tried to rub his shaft on Grushenka's belly. But it was kept firm in the hand of the bedmaid, who was not willing to let go of such a nice plaything.

Grushenka kept her legs close and pressed her knees so tightly together that they hurt, but Ivan struggled to get between. He moved a bit, got his strong hand between her thighs and with a sudden jerk, lifted her right leg high up, almost to her shoulder. He now got between her legs with his own and his prick rested firmly on top of her cunt. The resistance of the girl had made him hot, but what followed made his prick almost burst.

The moment the prick touched her, Grushenka lost her apathy and with a wild scream, started to fight. Ivan had his arms around her, the left one over her right shoulder, the right one in the middle of her back. The tight grasp and the weight of him could not be shaken off. But Grushenka could move her arse and her legs and she made ample use of these when the dangerous shaft came in contact with her love-nest. The Princess, who would have killed any serf not performing her orders, was highly delighted to see this struggle and slipped her hand under her chemise to give her itching tickler a soft caress with her fingers.

Ivan tried to find his way. He moved his right hand under the buttocks of the struggling girl. He lifted his own behind and tried by crafty pushes to find the entrance, but now the girl who had previously caressed his arse, again came to his help. She went around the couch and caught Grushenka's other knee which she forced up against Grushenka's shoulder and moved it so that the virginal love-hole lay unprotected and open. The other girl again got hold of the prick and directed its head to the rosy entrance. 'Now!' shouted all the watchers, and Ivan well understanding that he was at last in position, lowered his weapon with force. Pressing with his right hand against the girl's bottom, with one firm and slow stroke, he thrust the prick into the cunt up to the hilt. Grushenka let out a terrible cry. After that she lay still as a corpse. Ivan moved back and forth several times until passionately groaning, he felt he could not hold it any longer. He spent; raptuously, grimly, abundantly sending his fluid into her. His muscles relaxed; breathing heavily he lay on her, stupidly exhausted.

The Princess was furious, her maids disappointed. They had hoped to see a good, long fucking match, but it was over before it really started and all there was now were two motionless bodies on top of each other. Certainly there was nothing thrilling in that. 'Get out! You brute!' commanded the Princess. 'Get back to your stable and stay there. You serfs are even too supid to fuck.' But she looked with interest at his still stiff prick, which he now slipped slowly out of the pussy, covered with blood. Ivan collected his pants, dropped his head and left the room like a beaten man.

He did not dare to look up or to glance at Grushenka. She lay with a pale face like a corpse on the couch, the middle of her body still raised by the pillow under her, the blood trickling out of her wound besmearing her thighs and the pillow. She had fainted and one could see that she was quite ill. With dismay the Princess had had her carried up to her room.

What sort of girl was this—who could not even stand a poke? That was what she said to a lady at afternoon tea as she was relating the story and added that the silly peasants were too stupid for words. The lady was not of that opinion. She answered that she often arranged a party for some of her hand-maids and serf-men and that they put on very exciting shows, enjoying their fucking in all three ways. She promised to invite Nelidowa as spectator to such a party and the Princess graciously accepted.

Meanwhile, Grushenka was in her bed, taken care of by Katerina. Katerina was afraid this episode might lead to pregnancy, and though she knew how to handle an abortion, she was afraid Grushenka's figure might change and Grushenka had become very useful. The scenes the Princess used to make because of her try-ons had been avoided since Grushenka took her place as a model. Therefore Grushenka had been washed and cleaned and in spite of her protests a hot irrigation had been made with water into which Katerina had put a powder. Next a cold wet towel was put between her legs. It did not ease the pain in her torn cunt. She still had to overcome the shock which the rape had effected. She was allowed to stay in bed all the next day by the old housekeeper, who muttered, 'What a soft girl! What a soft girl!'

CHAPTER IV.

The weeks after her rape were perhaps the happiest of Grushenka's youth. At least she looked her best and became a ravishing beauty. She was awakened. Her days of dreaming were over and gave place to a lively vivacity and an ever good mood. Many times, full of hell, she played little pranks on the other girls and the tailors and was sometimes punished by having to stand in a dark corner or with a few strokes from the whip. They were not severe punishments. The girl had such an air of good hearted spirits and happiness about her that no one became really angry with her. The reasons for her change were as follows.

A few days after losing her maidenhood, she had had to show her mistress a new costume, a light blue, fluffy affair with many ribbons and laces. The Princess had liked it, and incidentally had ordered the girl to show her cunt. She wanted to see what changes had come from the fucking. Grushenka lifted the costume carefully in front, another girl spread the slit of her trousers open while the Princess took a good look. There was no change. Nelidowa was thinking that one poke might not effect a great change, but that if that pussy before her eyes should be used often, the rosy and thin lips would certainly become thick and vulgar. Hence the order to Katerina that Grushenka was to be poked daily and that Katerina should supply various men in order that the business be attended to properly.

Katerina disliked this new order, for which she could not imagine the reason, but what could she do? She moved Grushenka's bed to a separate room in the basement and after dinner, gave the girl her instructions. First she gave her a salve and ordered her to smear it every day after dinner into her tube. This salve was to kill the sperm. The irrigations, to be taken afterwards, would make doubly sure that she should not get an enlarged belly.

Presently she sent a stable boy to the girl's room, a redhaired, freckled, undersized man, who grinned with delight. The love-making of the servants was controlled, but once in a while they were allowed to do some fucking. It was not half enough and they always craved for the opportunity. Very often there was a love match between two serfs and they were sometimes allowed to marry, receiving from the master a shack and a bit of land that they had to till in addition to the land of the owner of the estate. More often, when some girl got pregnant, the master commanded one of his men to marry her.

It was always a feast to be allowed to fuck and it was usually done in the hay of the stables or somewhere in the fields. A good party in a bed and an order to give her the limit was a pleasure! When the news came to the stable, the men threw dice for the trick and the red-head was much envied when he won.

Grushenka was sitting uneasily on her bed; she held one hand over her breasts, the other one clutched her thin dress in front. With a pitiful voice she begged him not to take her, to spare her. The shock from Ivan's handling was still in her bones. But the red-head had other ideas. He threw his wooden slippers into the air, slipped out of his shirt and trousers, and assured the frightened girl that it should be as if it were his wedding night and that he would not need any help like Ivan. Nay, he'd do the job alone and quite thoroughly. As he stood before her, naked, his prick ready for the anticipated pleasure, she did not know what to do. She kneeled before him and implored him to let her be, but he instead took hold of her hair and pressed her face against his testicles and laughed aloud when she tried to struggle away. Then he lifted her bodily up and threw her on the bed.

'For the quick poke in the woods,' he said, 'It's all right with clothes on, but I'll have you nude, my little bride. It's so much nicer.'

He started to loosen the hooks of her skirt and to tear it off her. Grushenka felt that resistance would not do and that her garments would be torn, and that meant the whip, so she unbuttoned her blouse herself and got rid of her trousers, while her lover-by-command lauded her change of mind. When they lay belly on belly, Grushenka again begged and prayed. She was very beautiful and the red-head had no reason to hurt her. He promised to be careful and explained to her, being a nice chap, that it would not cause her any pain, that she would, in fact, like it and that if she followed his suggestions, they could both enjoy it profoundly.

The frightened girl promised to do all he said and he proceeded with great care. He tickled her pussy with the point of his shaft for a while and then inserted it by degrees, moving always a bit back and shuffling it in again, each time more, until his hair rubbed closely against her well shaven Mount of Venus. He then inquired whether it had hurt and Grushenka answered in a soft, wondering voice, 'Just a bit. Oh! Be careful.'

But it had not hurt her at all, it was just a funny feeling, not exactly exciting, but almost pleasing. He told her to move her arse slowly up and down, which she did, while he lay stiff and strong, until he started himself to heave and to push, finally forgetting himself and fucking quite to his heart's content. Grushenka did not answer his strokes, she was still afraid that it might hurt again. But she held her arms close to his back and when finally he came, she pressed her cunt firmly against his belly and felt something like satisfaction when his hot scum spread into her insides.

He had not had enough. He stayed in her bed joking with her. He played around with her breasts and her cunt, laughed to see that she was shaved and pinched her bottom, good-heartedly. She discovered with amazement that he got stiff again and she did not fight him off when he put his prick in anew; a prick which was not so strong and terrible now as it had been before. This time her fright was gone. She wondered: 'So that is what they call fucking.' She thought, 'Really, it's not so bad.' Still she did not get a thrill out of it, although it felt rather pleasant.

This time he had to work harder to get the load out of his

balls. She assisted him very little, although she caressed his back with her hand shyly, and tried to make her cunt as small as possible, so that the slippery machine down there could get as much friction as possible. After he had come, she started to move and to heave. She wanted something more now herself, but he slipped his tired love shaft out of her. She was tired and slept so soundly that they had a hard time getting her up next morning.

Every night after dinner, a man came to fuck her. Sometimes they were elderly and brutal and did not undress, just laid her over the bed and fucked and gave her a slap on the behind and disappeared. Sometimes, they were mere boys, who were shy and Grushenka had a great time teasing them and working them up and finally seducing them many times so that they walked from the room with weak knees.

Grushenka learned to love it. She could not say when she came for the first time, but after it had happened, she succeeded in getting the supreme thrill with every man; half a dozen times if she liked her partner. She learned how to make love and soon became a passionate lover. The male servants in the house who had tried her out, praised her with glittering eyes. What a girl! What figure! What a piece of arse! A volcano!

These were fine weeks, weeks of thrills, weeks during which her body filled out and her mind became clear, weeks without dreams, full of reality. She looked at other girls with searching curiosity. She learned from them about their love affairs, she studied her mistress with appraising eyes. Couldn't she manage to get a nice boy as a husband and a little house with some acres and have children too? Why not? She learned who was influencing the master and the mistress, she made plans, she laid eyes on one of the best body servants of the Prince and though she never spoke with him or had intercourse with him, she believed she had fallen in love with him. All that ended of a sudden, and it was again her mistress who affected the change, her mistress who was by right and law Grushenka's destiny.

Nelidowa used to start many things, give many orders, and forget about them again. Her mind wandered.

Everything that did not pertain to her lover (of whom we will have to speak later) was done in a haphazard way. But Nelidowa remembered one night when she came from the bedroom of her husband, after working over his prick for some time, that Grushenka had been her means for finding out how a cunt would change by fucking; so she sent for her.

Grushenka had had a quick and meaningless poke from an elderly man that night about an hour before, and was still awake when the hand-maid of Nelidowa came for her. She put a bed sheet around her shoulders and walked nude and bare footed to her Highness's bedchamber. (It must be remembered that all people, high or low, male or female, slept without nightshirts at that time, and it is said that Marie Antoinette, some fifty years later, was the first one to create the mode.) Nelidowa had just washed her pussy and sat naked before her toilet table, while one of her maids braided her long black hair into pigtails.

Nelidowa was in a good mood and told Grushenka to wait until her hair was done. In a few minutes, she took the nude girl on her lap. She inquired whether Grushenka had been poked daily, whether the pricks had been big and long, whether she had learned to fuck properly and whether she liked it. Grushenka answered automatically, 'Yes,' to every question. Then Nelidowa gently opened the girl's legs and examined her pussy.

There was no change to be seen. The little love nest was tender and innocent, as though it had never held big male machines. The lips were perhaps more red, and fuller, but still firmly closed and thin. The Princess opened them and fingered the girl, who quivered under this caress. The Princess moved her more towards her knees, opened her own legs a little and wondered at her own cunt, which was wide open with thick flappy lips. Apparently it was not fucking but the hand of nature which had made the difference between their cunts.

Everything seemed to go well and the Princess was about to send her double to bed again, but in her dissatisfaction with the imperfect loving she had received from her husband, she felt induced to play more with Grushenka's cunt. Her finger started to rub it more insistently, she fingered also the arse hole, and then went back to the pussy. Grushenka leaned closely on the shoulder of her mistress, put one arm around her and with her free hand, caressed Nelidowa's full breasts and nipples. She sighed slightly and prepared to come, wiggling her bottom as well as possible in this sitting position.

Just when Grushenka began to feel fine, the Princess got vexed that the girl should get a kick out of it, while she herself felt only that her cunt was bothering her. With her old meanness, she pinched Grushenka's pussy with her sharp finger nails, hurting the tender inner parts of the lips terribly. Startled and with a cry Grushenka leapt from the woman's lap holding the injured spot with her hands, instinctively ducking away from her mistress.

Nelidowa, upset by the girl's screams, her nerves offended, said the guilty one had to be punished. As she reached for a leather slipper, her eyes had a gruesome expression. She scolded the girl and made her lie down over her lap. Cracking slaps fell on Grushenka's backside and thighs, the pain shot in lightning heat with each stroke through her body. The slipper was merciless. Grushenka wiggled and kicked, cried and screamed, then subdued her cries to sobs. Her buttocks, her legs felt as if a red hot iron was being applied.

The struggling arse berore her eyes did not leave the Princess without feeling. She started to feel rather good, nay she felt keenly that her cunt got hot, and she acted accordingly. She let Grushenka fall to the carpet, then took hold of her head and forced it between her own opened legs. One of her hand-maids, seeing what was going on, rushed behind her mistress, embraced her breasts and coming with her arms from behind, drew her gently back, thus placing her in a position in which to enjoy herself.

Grushenka did not know what to do. She had, of course, heard that the Princess was sucked off by her bed-maids and she knew that some servant girls were supposed to do the same to each other. Lady's Love was at that time more common than it is today. It was an art practised with great finesse in the harems, and the Russian household was still very much like a harem.

Grushenka did not know exactly what was expected of her; no one had taught her these things. She was half suffocated by the passionate pressure with which the Princess forced her face against her open hole. She kissed or tried to kiss the hair around the entrance but kept her tongue in her mouth and only her lips rubbed and brushed over the battlefield. Nelidowa took that as obstinate resistance. She let her go and pushed her away with a firm kick of her bare feet. One of her bed-maids immediately took Grushenka's place (the girl said later she had done so to avert murder, so wild were the eyes of her mistress) and with apt and learned strokes of her tongue she brought the passionate young Princess to fulfillment. She came, groaning and moaning, cursing and mixing into the words tender expressions which were meant for her lover. Finally she closed her eyes and hung exhausted in the arms of the serf girl who held her. The bed-maids carried her to her bed and put her softly between the sheets. Grushenka slipped out of the room, hoping all would be forgotten the next day. She made up her mind to ask one of the girls how to satisfy the mistress in case she again should be called to this duty.

The next afternoon it was clear that Nelidowa had not forgotten. Katerina was ordered to appear with Grushenka. The Princess instructed briefly and without explanation, 'Give that girl fifty lashes with the cowhide and do it yourself and don't let her be fucked from now on.'

Katerina closed her lips tight. If she followed her mistress's order, the girl would be dead by sunset. She never could stand it. Men died with less than that number of blows. She led the trembling and loudly sobbing girl to the basement, where in a far corner a room for the punishment of the serfs was equipped with instruments of torture. Katerina led her to the whipping block and Grushenka, her eyes full of tears, stripped without resistance and laid herself over the saddle-like middle of the block. Katerina chained her arms and feet to rings. Then she questioned the frightened girl and Grushenka, her head hanging to the floor, related the happenings of the night before.

Katerina was thinking hard while she fingered the different whips to find one of lighter weight. She looked at the white body, stripped for punishment and at the whip and threw the whip away. 'Listen!' she said. 'One should not trust such a bitch as you are, but I will spare you if you can keep your mouth shut. Right after this you will go to bed and stay there for two days and be sick, and you'll tell everybody that I put a wet linen over you, so as not to blister your skin. If you do as I say, you'll get off lightly, because you did not know better and it was not your fault.' Whereupon Katerina hit her several times with her hard hand over the arse which did not hurt less than the slipper the night before. 'And one thing more. You are going to learn how to suck perfectly so that you know better next time. Understand?'

Katerina had something on her mind when she made this decision. Nelidowa was using up her maids in quick order and Katerina had always to supply new ones. The Princess, cruel and beastly as she could be (like many people who come from nothing into power) was equally good-hearted and carelessly friendly when she was in a good mood. None of her personal maids liked to stay long with her. The small leather whip with the golden handle was always too near and the moods of the mistress changed too quickly. The way to get away from her was to get married. They sometimes asked her for it outright and got what they wanted, including the men they had picked for themselves. Sometimes they did what they could to get pregnant and then they were scolded or even put for a few days in a dark room with water and bread. They were never severely punished (oriental women have a religious respect for a pregnant woman) and in the end were usually supplied with a husband. Then it was up to Katerina to find another maid; handsome, with a good figure, well trained in washing and clothing the mistress, alert, keen and also a good Lesbian.

The handmaids lived in one big room where, when not busy, they waited the call of the Princess. They passed their time telling lewd stories, playing with each other, indulging in sucking parties. They were ready for that always, because they wore only light Russian blouses with such a low neck that half of the breast was exposed and wide skirts with no other garments below. Bending down and pulling the skirt up offered the necessary position for the whip and lying down and pulling the skirt up made ready for a little play with the tongue.

After Grushenka had spent two lonesome days in bed, she was turned over to an efficient instructress of cunt lapping. Three or four young girls, not more than seventeen years of age were broken in by this woman, who was above thirty and understood her job well. The girls had to give each other a sucking, and then they had to show their ability to the teacher by working on her pussy. If it had not been for the fact that this teacher always had a switch in her hand, which she used when she was not satisfied, Grushenka would have enjoyed these instructions.

When she was put before the pussy of a young blonde girl and told to lick first around the lips, then to enter the vagina at the bottom and finally to concentrate on the clitoris, she liked it and was herself tickled by the movements of her tongue. Perhaps this was because this girl was very responsive, quivering with delight and passion under the tender tongue treatment. Grushenka also enjoyed it hugely when one of the girls got hold of her own pussy and she responded with such delight that the teacher had the execution stopped before she came. Grushenka did not mind. When her turn came to lick the cunt of this woman, she slipped unnoticed a finger on her own spot, and while rubbing herself to a climax, she gave the woman so amazingly strong a tongue licking that the elderly one then prophesied that she, Grushenka, would become a famous lover. Most of the peasants learn in time to satisfy even a refined lady's love, but they did so automatically; the vigour and that love which cannot be described was missing.

Grushenka was no more to be touched by men. The little divertisement she had while learning to be a Lady's Lover ceased quickly also. She was at a loss what to do to satisfy the passion which she had developed. Should she take a secret lover as many other girls did? There was the danger of being found out and having her bones broken on the rack. Should she start an affair with another girl? That again would lead to some terrible punishment. She tried her own finger, even stole a candle and played with herself in bed. It was not good, in fact she felt unhappy the next day and cried without reason. But while so far her life had been like that of most of the other girls, a new and exciting chapter was to begin for her.

CHAPTER V.

When Nelidowa went to bed for the first time with Alexey Sokolow she understood of a sudden what her marriage would cost her. She had known that His Highness, the Ex-Governor, her exhalted Prince-husband, was wealthy and she would have social position and power. But there, lying next to her like an orang-utang was the ugly body of the man who was now by right and law her master, mentally and physically. He was bald but had plenty of woolly hair around the lower part of his head, growing into a long thick beard reaching to his chest which was covered with thick black hair. His chest was enormously broad, his arms short and muscular with broad short hands, and he had an enormous belly with a tissue of muscles all around the waist line. His skin was dark, his thighs almost brown. He had small piercing suspecting eyes and a big mouth with the lower lip especially thick and sensual. His prick was short and thick and his balls betrayed at a glance that they held plenty of ammunition and loved the shooting game.

During the long stupendous wedding with a thousand new faces congratulating her, everybody bowing deeply before the Prince, who was in a jovial mood, she had been thrilled. He had seemed handsome clad in a brilliant blue uniform studded with glittering medals and buttons of real gold and with a snow-white wig with a long pigtail, which had dangled frivolously over the gold collar of his costume. He had worn high patent leather boots and rings with dazzling stones. It was thus that Nelidowa, the bride, had first seen her new spouse. She had been startled to fright when the cannons bellowed on their arrival at the palace and was moved to tears when the Arch-Bishop (think of it, a real Arch-Bishop performing the ceremony, and in her home

45

town, not even the lowest monk would listen to her confession) spoke the blessings for them. She had drunk it into herself, blinded with the splendour, and had made all kinds of good promises to herself. She had been in a trance, had kissed her new hand-maids and assured them heaven on earth when they undressed her late at night, and she had gone to her new husband (according to his orders quite nude) intending to thank and thank him, to tell him that she was going to be his chattel and his faithful wife. But when she lay next to him, when she observed how this Prince of the costly uniform had changed into an abhorrent brute, she had not been able to say a word.

Prince Alexey Sokolow did not expect a word from her. He had never thought of a woman as a human being but as his property. He owned many and kept dozens of serf girls always near his bedroom. He had them follow him on his voyages. He had had them since his father first ordered him to fuck a girl when he was sixteen years of age. He had never had an affair with a society girl, because she was somebody else's property. While he made many daring business ventures and acquired the estates of many men convicted for political or other reasons during his two score years as governor, women were something not to be taken illegally. If you liked a bitch, you could buy her; there was always a price which could be met.

During his trips to Western Europe, he had learned that there were harlots, whom one could buy for an hour or a day. He even brought to Russia with him some wenches who did a nice job in bed. It seemed money wasted, however, because his own slave girls could do as well and even better. They were harder, had no moods and were easily put in their places when they did not behave properly.

Alexey had no special love habits. He did not know about the refinements of copulation; he just wanted a good fuck. He wanted to put it in to his own satisfaction, regardless of the pleasure of his partner, and was satisfied when the arse moved up and down against him. That is, it had been so when he was younger and had not yet acquired his belly. Now he would not have been able to touch the spot with his machine had he laid himself on top of a girl. With his growing belly he had discovered a better position; the girl had to kneel straddle-legged over him and move up and down while he lay still, moving only the muscles of his enormous buttocks alternately. He also managed to give his shaft a to-and-fro movement without lifting his arse from the linen, because the muscles were well developed around his sex-organs.

He did not explain much of this to his bride. She really was stunning looking and he was well satisfied with this new acquirement to his bed assortment. He had not married her for love, and if she had not pleased him he would have fucked her once or twice (he liked to take maidenheads) and then probably forgotten her. But she was a good morsel and he was going to use her. He broke her in without further ado. He felt her over with his thick hands, he rudely forced his finger into her pussy, he pulled her on top of him, he spanked her bottom a bit, in short he first took possession of her with his hands.

Nelidowa tried to make it easy for herself by kissing him on the cheeks (with closed eyes) by snuggling against him (to her own disgust) and by not struggling when she felt his big finger enter her hole. Then with a jerk, holding her with his hands at the waist-line, he sat her with his powerful arms on top of his testicles. Nelidowa knew well what it was all about; a married girl friend had told her, so she understood that Master Prick, now cornered between her Venus Hill and the steep wall of his belly, had to go into the cage and she knew that it would hurt her. But she was not only required to stand for it, she had to put it in herself; she had, with her own weight, to tear that little piece of skin which is precious only to virgins. She did not have the nerve. She stared with fixed eyes at the brute who was lying below her, a few hours ago still an utter stranger and now entitled to defile her.

'Put it in and sit on it and fuck,' yelled Alexey to her. Poor Nelidowa. She took that hard instrument, so broad but still not so long, in her nimble fingers. She moved it towards the entrance and nervously lowered her bottom. But things needed a more vigorous handling. Alexey was prepared for that. He did not like to induce a woman to do this or that; he did not like to fumble. He had taken more vigins than one since his belly had grown. He had expected even more resistance from his bride and the usual preparation had been made.

He struck a little gong on his night table. Three servant girls rushed in. Before Nelidowa knew it, two had got hold of her with an expert grip: one hand went underneath each knee, took hold of it and stretching the leg as far from the middle of the body as possible, the other hands grabbed her shoulder. She was lifted up a bit and lowered down carefully. Meanwhile the third girl took the tail of her master with one hand, opened up with apt fingers the unused cunt, and saw to it that both met in the right way. She then commanded: PUSH, and both women, holding the Princess, gave a satisfactory pressure to her shoulders. Satisfactory, because Master Prick was in and had pierced the little membrane.

Nelidowa howled, the Prince moved his bottom, the girls let go of her knees and took hold her waist and shoulders and moved her up and down. It took about five minutes for the Prince to come.

The Princess received a washing and the master was likewise cleaned up from the blood. She had to lie down again along side of her master. 'You'll learn,' he said. 'And now we'll show you how the next part has to be done.' He bedded her head on his hairy chest, put her hand on his machine and told her to massage it tenderly. As she did so he groaned and snorted, his fat hand on her small bottom. It pleased him that her arse was small and her thighs straight and slim; when the girls were fleshy it was hard for him to bury his prick deep into their cunts.

After a while he was stiff again. The gong sounded a snappy order, and a serf-girl ready for work entered the room. She knew what to do. She mounted the master, so that her face was towards his feet and her back towards his belly. He put some more pillows under his head and managed to bend forward enough so that he could reach the behind of the girl, who was riding him with slow firm motions up and down. He lay perfectly still, his hand playing with her behind, and he found her arse hole and squeezed his finger in just as he came. After that he lay quietly and had himself washed with a wet towel.

He explained to his new wife that fuck number one was to be given with full front view; fuck number two reversed. He said that she was to come three times a week, that she was to learn her technique quickly and that she could now go back to her own bed-chamber, because he wanted to sleep. No good-night, no caresses, no good word for her. But also no bad word. He was instituting a routine which was kept from then on.

It was strictly kept because he liked her better than his slave girls and she soon learned how to squeeze out his prick properly with her pussy. Also it must be remembered that he paid more for her upkeep than for that of his other female retinue. Nelidowa did not mind the prick so much; she simply closed her eyes and managed to come and to get a thrill. What she could not stand was the play of his strong hands over her body before every jump, especially between the first and the second fucking, when he wanted to heat himself up again. At this time, he hurt her quite often. He fussed around with her breasts, pinched the nipples and laughed when she tried to avoid him. When he toyed with her love nest, he did not begin with any gentle play around the entrance, warm up the tickler and then intrude into the tube. No, he just pushed his finger rudely in as deep as he could, crooked it and rubbed it. It always gave her pain and a shock. But she did not complain and even gave him gentle words and told him how happy she was. It was the price demanded of her and she gave it.

The rest of their personal relations were also regulated by rules. They ate apart, except when they had guests. They went to all social affairs together and he liked to show her off and sent her for such occasions, jewellery from the seemingly endless store of his iron chest. He spoke politely to her, in few words, and never told her about his own affairs. For example, she did not know that he had big estates in the

49

South, until they travelled over them. He confided his affairs only to an old trusted man-servant and to very few of his friends. He was a man of few words, used to command and he exercised his will with great determination.

Nelidowa had to find her life with her women friends. She chatted with her bed-maids and amused herself as she could with anything that was proper and becoming for the wife of a great Prince. He never beat her, as many husbands did their wives, and he never lost his temper. He had resorted to the lash only a few times in his life, sending the culprit to the stable master for the punishment. However, when he was seriously dissatisfied, he would have the guilty person stand while he smacked the face a few times.

He did this to his wife on occasions when her giddiness had aroused the mockery of other society people and he had heard of it. When he heard that she was beating her maids or had them beaten, he discussed it briefly with her. He said that she had the right to do so, but that if one of the servants should become seriously ill or die on account of the punishment, he would then inflict the same torture on her. 'They are my property,' he added, 'As well as you are.' That closed the incident because he remembered that his mother had whipped her maids also.

He had expected to have a child from the Princess; he wanted an heir to cheat his relatives. She remained barren. He had a few virgins come from one of his estates, fucked them and held them under strict watch, so that they could not sleep with other men. Out of four girls, two became pregnant. Therefore it was Nelidowa, not he, who was at fault. But he decided not to take another wife. Not because he could not have got rid of her or because he loved her, but that it was not so important after all. She was there and she could remain there.

After the first year of her marriage, feeling secure now as a Princess and a powerful man's wife, Nelidowa was ripe to take a lover. He must be distinctly different from her husband, a bit exotic, maybe a Frenchman. As it turned out, he was a Pole. Gustavus Swanderson, he made known, was his name. He came from Warsaw, where his father had a

50

string of disorderly houses. Gustavus, who then bore the name of Boris, managed, during a raid on his father's establishments, to get hold of some gold which the old man kept hidden. With this, he travelled to Sweden, changed his name, bought the patent of an officer and played the nice chap for the ladies. He was decidedly romantic, with a wealth of brown hair, elegant in his movements, enterprising, and not altogether a bad boy. His hobby was drawing and his satirical sketches of society people were quite the thing. He started to learnt architecture, first just to play with it, but later became interested and took part in the erection of some military buildings and forts. When Peter the Great was already quite elderly, he came to Russia and offered his services as a builder. Peter, though not much impressed with him, sent him to Moscow where a big bridge was under construction and here he began to be a slight success in his line.

When he met Nelidowa he was around thirty years of age, ten years her senior. He was different from the other men; his skin was white, he was not hairy, his hands were fine, almost feminine and tender. He kept himself clean and modish and his laughter was of a romantic sadness. Nelidowa selected him for herself at first sight. The man had very little choice as to whether he wanted her or nor. He had to conquer her because she wanted him. Oh, she fixed it in a very romantic way. Poems fluttered through the air; secret words passed, only understood by the conspirators. Nelidowa played her part wonderfully, with tears and resistance and with faked fainting spells.

She won him and she was very satisfied. He was so tender, so full of caresses, so loving, so romantic and when, after long kissing and playing and toying, she finally felt his hot rod enter her hungry crevice, she nearly fainted with delight. Of course, when he built lovely castles in the air about elopement and how they would live in Paris as happy as doves, she listened like a happy but already grown up child to a smartly told fairy tale. While she avoided saying 'No', in her heart she never considered him more than a lover. Something necessary to a woman's life, but not to be mixed up with the reality of a Princess.

On the other hand, this reality bothered her three times a week when she walked nude, except for blue slippers, through different rooms to the bed of a big brute who offended her body and for whom she was nothing but an instrument for prick-massage. She could not pretend she had a head-ache or did not feel well, because if she did, her husband would send a servant with a brief message that he was not fucking her head but her cunt. As long as she did not have her monthly, she had to appear. No pity from that quarter and no excuse accepted.

Another incident occurred which proved to be annoying. Gustavus fell in love with her and the longer the liaison lasted the more enamoured he became. With this his jealousy developed, and while the brutal and elderly Prince in his strength entertained no slightest thought that his wife might be unfaithful, Gustavus, in his tender and weak constitution, was crazed with jealousy. She had once described to him in what way she had to fuck her husband and though this was still early in their affair, he was near to assassinating his rival. Lately he had pestered her to refuse to play the dutiful wife and in passionate words had threatened to take the life of the Prince and even hers. She told him she would do as he wished and, lying, said she did not go to her husband since at present he had a passion for one of the serf girls. Gustavus did not believe her fully and they had many scenes. She did not want to give up her lover. She could not stay away from her master. She had to think her way out.

Suddenly she was struck with an idea: didn't they tell her that Grushenka looked just like her, not only in figure but in face also? It was whispered that they were like twins, that nobody could really say who was who. If that was true then Grushenka could take her place in the bed-chamber of her spouse. This thought was so daring, so exciting, that she had to go to work right away. She commanded Grushenka to her presence and had herself and the girl clothed in dresses exactly similar and their hair done in the same way. She then had one of her maids ask other servants from the basement which of the two was the Princess. The servants looked uneasy, afraid to make a mistake. They tried to avoid a direct answer and finally pointed at random, missing the Princess as often as they chose her. That was fine! All that was now needed was for the Princess to teach Grushenka exactly how to behave with the master.

She dismissed all the servants including her hand maids, locked herself in her bedroom with Grushenka and made her kneel down and swear solemnly never to betray her. She confided her plan to the girl and rehearsed to the smallest detail the way the fucking parties took place. When Grushenka undressed, an obstacle appeared: Grushenka was clean shaven around the pussy. There was nothing to do but to wait until the hair had grown. So it was decided. During this time, for many an afternoon, Grushenka was told how she would have to behave during the coming fucking parties and Nelidowa, during this period, observed herself in all details when she was with her mate. She was sure of success. The bedroom of the Prince was lit by a single large candle which stood in a corner far from the bed and there was a small candle in front of the Ikon. This small illumination would not have permitted him to find out the difference between Nelidowa and Grushenka even if they had not been so much alike.

Another remark must be made concerning these confidential rehearsals between the young women. They began to like each other. The Princess had never thought of Grushenka before except as a low and silly serf girl. Now she wanted something from her. She ordered her, of course, to take her place. Grushenka could tell the master and the catastophe arising from such a mishap would have been unthinkably awful! Therefore the Princess became kind to the girl, chatted with her and tried to discover her character. She was captivated with Grushenka's simple charm and faith. On the other hand, Grushenka now learned that the Princess was unhappy, uncertain of herself, that she had had a hard youth, that she longed for kindness and that her nervous and brutal behaviour did not arise from coldness, but from unawareness. Grushenka became a hand-maid of her mistress, was always around her, was her confidante in her love matters and her companion during the long hours of the dragging days. The whip was never applied to her, she was not scolded, and she slept next to her mistress's room and became something like a little sister.

When Grushenka's hair had grown, (they examined it daily) the day came when a male servant announced that his Highness expected the visit of her Highness. Grushenka put on the blue slippers and both women walked through the several rooms to the master's chamber. Grushenka entered while Nelidowa, with beating heart, peeped through a crack of the door. The Prince had come from a card game where he had been drinking and felt tired and a little lascivious. Grushenka held his stub in her hand, worked it firmly, mounted the horse and worked his machine into her tube. For quite a time he could not come on account of the liquor he had drunk but she came herself once or twice (she had not fucked for ever so long) until he groaned and moved his arse and was through. He was through for the night and sent her away with a slap on the behind.

Nelidowa took Grushenka with her to her bed. She was excited, joyously excited, while Grushenka was very calm. She had done the whole job without hesitation. She wanted to help her mistress. That was her duty; for the rest, she was not concerned. Nelidowa hugged and kissed the girl and aroused by the fucking she had seen, had two hand maids come in to give herself and her friend (as she said now for the first time) a good sucking.

So it was that Grushenka became the master's wife as far as his bed was concerned. The first few times Nelidowa went with her to the door and peeped. After that she remained in the bed until Grushenka returned and a few weeks later was no longer concerned about the matter. When the servant came to announce that his master's prick was ready (that was the sense of the message) Nelidowa would say she'd come right away, and Grushenka who lay on the bed in the next room, got up, went to the Prince, fucked, washed her pussy and went back to sleep.

Until that time Nelidowa had satisfied the whims of her mate in spite of her repulsion. She now found her satisfaction under the pushing of Gustavus' considerate shaft while Grushenka had to look forward to the short but thick prick of her master. Grushenka had never known fine people, so the rudeness of the Prince did not shock her. On the contrary his brutal force and immense vitality captured her and made her forget the repulsion which his belly might have inspired. She loved his sceptre. She began not only to massage it, but to caress it, to kiss it and she soon began to suck him. He thought first that she wanted a gift from him, perhaps one of his estates or a will made out in her favour. But when no such demands came, he felt with pleasure what a passionate, refined and loving wife he had.

Grushenka had a much easier time with him than Nelidowa used to have. The Princess always used to aggressively try to stop him from taking hold of her body with his hands, but now the Prince was stiff before Grushenka was in bed and she sat on him before he could annoy her with his hands. Besides, she fucked with so much passion that she did not mind when he squeezed her nipples while his machine was in her pussy. During the intermission, he lauded her with teasing words about her newly found temperament but hardly touched her, waiting until she would take hold of his prick again. She someimes lay between his legs, raising his big behind with a pillow, and licked his dark brown balls with intense ardour, the hard strong smell of his balls and the odour of his rim was a sensation to her nostrils. She quivered all over and got immensely excited and worked herself up by pressing her legs close together. She did not want to follow his orders to come up and mount him; she wanted to make him come with her lips, to drink the liquid, but he never let her.

Sometimes Nelidowa would watch this scene out of curiosity, jealous that the girl enjoyed it so much. Afterwards she would pinch her and scold her about something and then again she would kiss the girl's mouth, lick her lips and teeth, because she felt the contamination of the sex excitement which had got hold of Grushenka. Sometimes she would decide to go to her husband herself, but at the last moment she would change her mind, and go to her lover. If he were not in the neighbourhood, she would have one of her maids satisfy her caprice.

All went well except for some small incidents. For example, the master would tell Grushenka something he wanted done the next day and she, not familiar with the people concerned or with the facts, would have a hard time remembering exactly what he had said. Or the Princess would be asleep when she came from the master's bedroom and she would lie awake the whole night so as not to forget. At other times, Grushenka would have a rash or pimples on her face which Nelidowa did not have, and she would be much afraid of detection in spite of the subdued light in his bedchamber.

Nelidowa told her lover the huge joke she had played on her mate and smuggled him into her own bed room and prepared with care the comedy of watching the fucking party of her husband with Grushenka. When Gustavus arrived, she presented Grushenka to him and made him compare them to find out who was who. To her great satisfaction, he was not for a moment in doubt although they wore no clothes. The reason for his quick judgement was that Nelidowa alone spoke, while Grushenka kept silent with a smile on her lips. She wanted to please Gustavus of whom she had heard so much; she had a romantic affection for him through Nelidowa.

Grushenka liked Gustavus as soon as she laid eyes on him. He was so gracious in his movements, his bearing was elegant, his hands were white, fine and well taken care of, in great contrast to those of the Russian men. He was eager to point out differences between the two: a little mole underneath the shoulder blade, the different shape of the bust, the flavour of the hair. Of course 'his love' was more beautiful. Though this pleased her, Nedidowa had to show him that she was the mistress and Grushenka the slave. First she told him what a pig Grushenka was for liking the prick of the Prince and sucking him off, then she turned Grushenka around and around, exposing her in every fashion. Finally she pinched the girl and suggested that Grushenka prove her art by kissing his shaft, but Gustavus, ashamed of all this play, refused.

Just then a message came from the Prince, who expected the Princess. Grushenka moved her hand over her bust and belly as if she were stroking her skin, she lightly rubbed her pussy with her fingers and opened the lips a few times just to have everything ready. She then stepped into the little blue slippers and went towards the bedroom of the Prince-husband. Nelidowa and Gustavus followed. Tip-toeing quietly, they took posts at the crack of the door.

Grushenka, well aware of the watchers and annoyed by the humiliation to which Nelidowa had submitted her, did not follow the usual behaviour. The lovers at the door could see the Prince on a bed with light blue silk covers, resting on his back, his fingers playing a happy rhythm on the bed sheet, his lips sensually pursed; the picture of a man who knows that he will be taken care of shortly. The door through which the lovers peeped was toward the foot of the bed, and his monstrous hairy body and big belly were plainly visible.

Grushenka leaned over and took in her left hand the big balls, caressing them while reaching underneath them and playing with her finger in his rim. Meanwhile her right hand held his prick, which she massaged. The prick was half asleep but with good inclination to wake up. The gentle treatment soon made the machine stiff. Grushenka did not kiss it; she pointed maliciously with her tongue in its direction and smacked her lips, but she did not embrace the shaft with them.

Instead, she mounted. The lovers could clearly see how she held the prick with two fingers of her right hand, how she opened her cunt with the left hand, and how Master Priapus slowly poked his nose into her love-nest. Grushenka bent forward, and giving over her splendid breasts to his grasping hands, made a few firm and deep up and down movements.

Then of a sudden, she bent back. Opening her knees as wide as possible, getting a deep hold of his machine with her cunt, she leaned so far back that her elbows almost touched her own heels. Of course the fat master was unable to reach any part of her body in this position, and groaning with excitement, he swore at her to bend forward. He used all the curse words he knew and his short arms waved with helpless strokes through the air. It was a funny picture; the riding girl with a determination on her face to squeeze his prick out with her cunt, and the pinioned monster who had to submit to his excitement, though mad to reach her. It was so funny a picture that Nelidowa and Gustavus could not restrain their giggles. Until this had happened, they had stood close together, Nelidowa holding his prick while his fingers fondled her love nest. When Grushenka had engulfed the Prince's shaft, they had keenly felt their own sex excitement.

The Prince was startled. Who was at the door? He moved and was about to throw his fair rider off to investigate. Grushenka, sensing the danger, threw herself forward and pressing him into the cushions with her weight, began to love up his face and head with kisses and the caresses of her hands. This brought about his crisis. He came with all his force and was unable to do anything but squirt his sperm into her. Thus the lovers had time to escape. Of course, the second party when Grushenka was riding the other way around, could not be observed by them, but, as by that time Nelidowa was already squirming under the pressure of her beloved 'soldier' perhaps it did not matter much.

CHAPTER VI.

When Prince Sokolow was on one of his estates, the Princess usually contrived to have Gustavus as house guest with them. The Prince was usually building and constructing and Gustavus had become his architect. Therefore there was no reason for misconstruing his presence. The Princess went to her lover's room as soon as Grushenka was with her husband. Great precaution was taken to prevent detection, lest their idyll be destroyed. But in Moscow it was very dangerous to smuggle Gustavus nightly into the palace, so he took a suite not far from the Sokolows, and Nelidowa stole out of the house at night by a small back door and visited him. That is what she had done one night, the dramatic events of which will now be told.

The Prince and Princess had been to a ball. They came home together, she gaily talking; he as usual, saying little. He told her to come to him as soon as she was ready. Entering her room, the Princess called Grushenka and while she changed from her ball gown to a simple street dress, not forgetting to put some perfume under her arms and between her legs, Grushenka left for the bedroom of the Prince. Soon afterwards, Nelidowa departed from the palace.

The first encounter between Grushenka and the Prince took place as usual. Grushenka was a bit lazy and tired that day. In fact she had been sleeping before the couple came back from the ball. But she Frenched him all right and rode his prick afterwards, quite a long ride this time because both of them seemed, somehow, without desire. Having accomplished her aim, she stretched herself alongside of him and started mechanically to play with his testicles preparing for the second encounter.

The Prince began, in a muttering way, a conversation.

'How did you like the diamond necklace which the Countess of Kolpack was wearing tonight?' he asked.

'Ah! Splendid!' replied Grushenka indifferently.

'Do you intend to go to the tea-party of Countess Kolpack?' continued the man.

'Maybe I will. Maybe I won't,' Grushenka said, trying to imitate the nonchalant ways of her mistress and getting intensely interested in her master's balls. But to her great surprise and fright, the Prince sat suddenly upright, put his one hand on her throat and with the other seized her hair.

'Who is the Countess Kolpack?' he shouted. 'Who is she? Who is she?' Such a countess, in fact, did not exist.

'Well, well—' was all Grushenka could mutter under his grip. She felt the game was up. She felt that the question had been a trap. She knew everything was lost. It was. One of his man-servants had told all to the Prince, who had investigated carefully and learned everything, even knew that at this very minute his cheating wife was in the arms of her lover. But he wanted to make sure. He wanted the facts first hand.

'Who are you? Don't lie!' he cried into Grushenka's face, lessening his grip to give her an opportunity to speak.

'Who am I—' stuttered the frightened serf-girl. 'Well, don't you know your own wife? Have you lost your mind? God forgive me!' and she crossed her heart in great anguish.

The gong sounded. The servant, prepared in advance, came in. Grushenka was seated on a chair. The Spanish shoes were brought in and put on her feet. The wooden edges of this instrument, invented during the Inquisition, pressed painfully against the flesh and bones of her nude feet even before the servant started to turn the screws. The Prince stopped him. He addressed her, almost formally, asking her again to confess who she was. She kept her mouth shut. She bit her lips. A motion from the Prince and the servant made the first turn. Her feet went numb. The second turn—the pain shot up her body. Screaming, she twisted in her chair, trying to liberate herself. She was mad with fright and pain, even though the wood had actually not yet cut her skin.

Then she gave in. She promised to confess everything; the

screw was unloosened, so was her tongue. In a stream of tears, she confessed. When she came to the end, she threw herself at the Prince's feet and begged for mercy, not for herself, but for her poor mistress. He just frowned at her incoherent utterances. He told the servants to lead her away as arranged in advance.

She was taken howling and screaming to the torture chamber in the basement. Large torches were lighted. She was put on a chair with two arms but no back. Her arms, from the elbows to the wrists, were fastened to the arms of the chair; a leather strap secured her tightly to the corners of the seat. After the two male serfs had done this job, they were uncertain what to do next. They felt her all over, had their jokes with her and discussed whether they should put their pricks in her mouth.

While Grushenka had been in the service of her mistress and taken her place with the master, none of the serfs dared to touch her. But now she seemed doomed. Why shouldn't these servants make her suck them off before her bones were broken on the rack? For that was, in their opinion, the least the master would do. Uncertain as the whole affair was, however, they decided to nap until further orders were forthcoming, and they stretched themselves on the floor in a half sleep.

Grushenka looked around. She had plenty of time to observe the gruesome room. Next to her stood a chair similar to the one she was strapped to. All kinds of handles and machinery were underneath the seat, but she could not make out what they were for. In the middle of the room was the flogging block over which she had been laid by Katerina, the most used instrument in the room, a kind of saddle on four legs with rings and ropes on it to tie the delinquent in the most receptive position. One wall was covered with all kinds of beating instruments: knouts, leather straps, whips and the like. On the next wall were the racks; ladder-like frames against which the culprit was fastened, while light and heavy bats stood around with which legs or arms could be broken. Chains and hanging racks, on which the man or woman to be punished was hung in such a way that the arms were twisted backward, completed the outfit of the room, a replica of which existed in the houses of all the masters of that time.

While Grushenka observed all these terrors, Prince Sokolow acted according to his plan. He dressed in a Russian blouse and high boots. He had his servants pack his trunks. He then went down to the back entrance through which Nelidowa was to come home. He took a low stool and sat down, watching the door. He sat thus for many hours, motionless, staring at the door, not closing or even blinking an eye. Dawn came, and with it Nelidowa. She entered with light steps in a happy and satisfied mood after a good fucking party with her lover. As soon as she closed the door, the short and tremendously strong Prince sprang at her, lifted her high in the air and flung her over his shoulder, her head and the upper part of her body dangling on his back. She uttered a piercing cry. She struggled to liberate herself, not knowing who had seized her. He carried her swiftly to the chamber where Grushenka sat.

'Tear the clothes from her body and strap her to that chair!' he commanded the serfs, throwing her in their direction. The Prince sat down on a low bench and waited for his order to be carried out. This was not very easy, for Nelidowa put up a terrific battle. She swore at the servants, she hit with her fists, she bit, she kicked—all to no avail. Her clothes were torn from her body, one man holding her hands against her back, while the other one removed one garment after the other. First came the skirt, then the trousers and the stockings. As soon as the lower part of her body was naked, one slave put his head between her legs. Holding her feet, he raised himself up and stood straight, so that she hung on his back, her spot right on his neck. The other man took a short knife, cut open her sleeves from the wrist to the shoulders, then did likewise to her blouse and chemise.

She was nude. They fastened her on the chair the same way they had Grushenka, and one of the men, with a bow, announced to the Prince that they were finished. The Prince ordered them from the room.

Nelidowa understood the situation perfectly by this time.

62

But with a haughty air she demanded that she be set free immediately, shouting that he had no right to punish her like that squealing brat, that serf girl next to her; that it was his fault and not hers that she had deceived him, because he was a brute, a monster with whom no decent woman would sleep. She told him that he was repulsive to her, that she despised him, that if she had not found this substitute she would have left him openly—and so on. In her rage she made a full confession about her love for Gustavus and that she was going to marry him as soon as she was rid of her tormenter.

The Prince did not reply. He inspected the nude women, amazed at their likeness. He felt no pity in his heart, not for them and not for himself. He knew her confession without having to listen to it. It was true! She had deceived him. Everybody but he had known it a long time. She had defied him doubly; put a serf girl in his bed while she fucked with her lover. A huge joke on himself. It had to be punished thoroughly.

He first went behind Grushenka's chair. He turned a handle. The seat on which the girl was sitting lowered itself down. Through holes in the seat came wooden nails, the points sticking upwards. Grushenka felt them pierce the flesh of her buttocks. At the same time the arms of the chair gave way while she tried frantically to get a hold of them. The braces of the arms fitted into tubes and she could not hold her weight on them. Her feet did not reach the floor, she sat on the nails and her own weight was driving them slowly and with increasing pain into her tender flesh. The Prince stepped behind the chair of his wife and unloosened here also the bolts which held the seat and the arms. After that he went with slow steps to the wall and took down a short leather strap and turned to his wife.

'I should burn your cunt which betrayed me and your mouth which just now besmirched me, with hot irons to mark you forever,' he said in a low voice. 'I will not do so. Not because I love or pity you, but because I understand that you are branded for life with a more terrible stigma. You are a low creature, not born to be a Princess. It was my error that I

63

took you and I beg you to forgive me—' He made a low bow while she sneered at him— 'but you must be punished in order to know who the master is.' Those were his only words to his wife and were the last he ever spoke to her.

With firm strong lashes of his muscular arms, he now began to whip her. He started with her back, laying stroke after stroke from her shoulders down to the lowest part of her body. The lashes hissed through the air. Nelidowa yelled and cried. She was unable to hold still. The points of the nails tore her bottom and cut the flesh more and more when she twisted around under each stroke. Her back, of which she was so proud, was covered with welts, but the Prince was not yet satisfied. He now began in front, hit her feet, her legs, stood before on an angle and hit into the full length of her thighs. He beat her belly and—without fury or hurry—finished up by laying cutting lashes over her breasts. He stopped only after he found her whole body was a mass of bruises.   Nelidowa did not cease to yell and cry and Grushenka mingled her own outcries with those of her mistress, not only because the nails bit into her bottom, but also out of compassion. She expected the same treatment but Sokolow resolved otherwise. He threw the whip away, came very close to her, looked into her fear-stricken eyes, and said, 'You did wrong. I am your master. You should have told me the first time.'—and he gave her two good smacks in the face as he would have done to a servant who had forgotten something. He left the room and slammed the door behind him.

There the two women sat on the nails, not knowing what the future had in store. Nelidowa cursed Grushenka and promised to roast her to death as soon as she could lay hands on her. She howled in her pain and tried to faint. Grushenka wept softly and avoided moving her body to lessen the pain from the nails. The torches burnt slowly down. The room became dark. The sobbing and wailing cut through the dark silence.

The Prince ordered a carriage. He went to Gustavus' house. He was bent on action. He aroused a sleeping servant, pushed him aside, strode into Gustavus' bedroom, which was already filled with the first morning light, and awakened the soundly sleeping Adonis with a punch in the face. Gustavus jumped out of his bed. The Prince pointed a pistol at the naked form of his rival. He demanded: 'No words are necessary between us. If you want to say a prayer, I will give you the time for it.'

Gustavus was wide awake. He was a squeamish Adonis, but he saw there was no escape. He stood upright, folded his arms over his chest and faced the stocky man in front of him. His white, slender body was motionless. The Prince took careful aim and shot him through the heart. Leaving, he tossed a purse of gold to the scared man-servant who cowered in the hall.

'Here,' shouted the Prince, 'Take that money and see to it that your master gets a decent funeral. Harlequins like him might not leave even enough money for that.'

His next stop was at the main police station. He aroused the drowsing lieutenant in charge and reported with sharp words: 'I am Prince Alexey Sokolow. I just killed with one shot Gustavus Swanderson. He was the lover of my wife. The whole city will confirm that, I am sure. The police will not prosecute me or I will chase my dogs at their throats. You know that! Report my word to the policemaster anyway. I leave for France today. I expect to have the policemaster as my guest when I come back. Report that to him. I will first call on the Czar in Petersburg to get leave of absence from him. (Here the voice of the Prince became threatening and the lieutenant understood him perfectly well.) If the policemaster wants to do anything about this affair, have him send a report to the Czar.' With that he strode out of the room.

Next he drove to his nephew, a lieutenant in a cavalry regiment. The orderly did not want to let the Prince enter his superior's apartment, but when he mentioned his name the soldier stood back in awe. Sokolow opened the curtains of the bedroom and the sun disclosed the sleeping lieutenant in close embrace with a girl. She woke up first and was a sight. Her make-up was smeared over her face by the night's love making, her bust was drooping, her legs were bent. She was a little Jewish whore who slept with the lieutenant for a few copecks. He loved his prick but he had no money to buy himself a good-looking sleeping partner. He was a lighthearted boy of twenty-five, slightly dumb, good looking and with a fine physique. He was deeply in dept. His rich uncle had never given him a penny or lent him his influence, because Sokolow disliked him as he did the rest of his family. But he was his nearest kin and had to be treated differently now.

Disregarding the bitch in the bed and all questions and objections of the aroused lieutenant, the Prince forced him to dress and accompany him, while the girl settled back under the covers with a yawn. The Prince drove with his nephew, who was very startled by the intrusion, to the house of his lawyer. He rang the bell and sent the sleepy servant upstairs to demand that the lawyer get dressed and come down at once. They sat in the coach, waiting. The uncle perfectly calm in his manner, drumming with his fingers; the nephew nervously apprehensive, trying in vain to learn what it was all about. Finally the lawyer joined them and they drove back to the palace. Prince Sokolow took them to his library, put paper and ink before the lawyer and dictated a complete power of attorney in favour of his nephew, instituting him as master of his whole estate until this granted power should be revoked. He demanded certain moneys sent to his banker in Paris; made a codicil to his will, dividing his estate and leaving the greater part to his nephew, who did not trust his ears. After that he dictated to the lawyer the summary of a divorce action against his wife, claiming infidelity and disowning her entirely. Then he ordered vodka and tea, walked with firm steps from one corner of the room to the other and explained to his amazed audience exactly what had happened.

He told his nephew that he hoped that in the future he would not sleep with such awful harlots, especially since he would find such a fine assortment of Russian girls available on his estates and would not need to soil his body on low whores. He dismissed both men, ordering his nephew to take leave of his regiment, to straighten out his small affairs and to return immediately to take charge. So and so much had to be earned by the estate during a year and if he should find on his return that things were not in shape, he would disown him again. The men left the lieutenant with a startled feeling of joy in his heart.

Two travelling carriages were now made ready for departure. The Prince went down to the basement where a crowd of women were in a flutter. They all knew what had happened. Grushenka had fainted, but Nelidowa was still wailing as she hung broken in the chair. The Prince sent for her hand maids. He had both women unstrapped and brought up to Nelidowa's room. Grushenka was revived and sent to her bed. The Prince ordered Nelidowa to get dressed. When they tried to put the chemise and the trousers on her, she screamed in pain because her lacerated body could not endure the touch of the linen. Nevertheless they put a dress on her and did it quickly because the staring look of the Prince made them hurry.

When Nelidowa was ready, they carried her to one of the carriages. The Prince ordered three of his most trusted men to enter the carriage also. He told them they were to drive her home to her aunt's, not to stop on the way, and to feed her in the coach.

'Let her shit in her trousers,' he added, 'but don't let her leave the carriage for a second. She is your captive and if you don't follow orders, I shall have you killed.'

The carriage drove on. It is not said what became of Nelidowa, nor do we know what became of the Prince, except that his divorce was granted and that he returned to his estate, as the records of his divorce trial prove.

CHAPTER VII.

Leo Kirilowicz Sokolow, the nephew, left the palace drunk with happiness. He, the unimportant little lieutenant, indebted, bound by the discipline of his regiment, short of everything that makes life wonderful for a young man, had suddenly become rich. Yes, he was independent, the master of a hundred thousand, maybe even a million souls. How should he know how many? He was a man now who would sit in council, be courted by the ladies, govern a huge estate. Of course his power was only temporary, only for the time Uncle Alexey was in Western Europe. But who could tell, the old bugger might die soon. In all events let the present be the present!

Things went so swiftly for this young man on this day that it is hard to detail even a part of them. Paul, the orderly, was kissed by his young master on both cheeks. The Jewish whore was pulled out of the bed by one leg, while Leo laughed like mad, and, after she had covered her meagre body with her rags and was leaving the barely furnished room, she felt something strike her on the back and fall to the floor. An oath on her lips, she picked it up automatically. It was a purse full of rubles, the total wealth Leo commanded before his uncle got him out of bed. The whore fled from the room clutching her unexpected wages of sin to her stomach and followed by the hilarious laughter of the young man.

In turn, the adjutant of the regiment, the captain and the colonel were notified of his resignation. Comrades were invited to a drinking bout at the palace that same evening. His scanty belongings were shipped over to the magnificent home of the Sokolows.

The new master started immediately to learn about his new household by questioning the various head servants. He sought advice on the administration of his estates by conferring with lawyers and men holding public office. He even sent messengers to all the head administrators in the provinces, mostly trusted serfs, inviting them to a conference on some future date. In short he plunged headlong into the task of his new responsibilities.

During the banquet that night he got so drunk that four men had to carry him to his bed where he collapsed unconscious. The palace itself would have been under great peril of demolishment by his no less sober friends had not one of them suggested a visit to a famous whore house.

When Leo awoke late the next day, his trusted orderly was at hand to nurse his tremendous headache with ice and herring. All the wealth in the world was then of no meaning to our Leo whose rebellious stomach chained him to his bedchamber. But early the next morning found him in the saddle on the back of one of the magnificent horses of his uncle's stables and he rode around inspecting his land. As he rode he began to collect his mental balance. The whole story of his young aunt and her substitute was certainly the best stroke of luck that ever could have happened, but it was not yet quite clear to him how it had all come about. Hence his order when he came back to the palace that he wanted to dine that night 'a deux' with Grushenka, and that she was to be clothed exactly like his aunt would have been for a great evening party.

Grushenka, after she had been lifted out of the nail chair, had been cared for by the other serf girls. They put sour cream on her offended behind, gave her cold water to drink and she fell into a feverish slumber which after a while became sound sleep. In fact, just as the above mentioned order was given she was getting out of bed and her buttocks, although still covered with scratches and red puncture marks, did not hurt anymore. She felt fit except for the anguish of wondering about what further punishment awaited her. She learned with great concern the fate of Nelidowa and Gustavus and the sudden departure of the old Prince. The message from her new master and the description of him—a nice young chap with a pointed black moustache, fresh eyes and a leaning toward drunkeness—was the sole theme of the conversation between her and the other maids.

Early in the afternoon they started to prepare Grushenka, putting on her the finest silk shirt of the Princess, a pair of laced trousers, silk stockings, high gilded shoes and an evening gown of light blue-silver brocade which left the breasts bare up to the nipples. Boris put on her with much earnestness and care a formal white wig with many ringlets. Her fingers and toe nails were perfectly manicured. A mild perfume was sprayed on her. Everyone of the handmaids did her best to make Grushenka as beautiful as possible as though she were a bride prepared for her wedding night. There was much speculation but very little doubt that the young master would fuck her. All the maidens in the house were eager to know about that and wished that they themselves might some fine day be the bed-fellow of the new Prince.

Grushenka entered the dining room flushed with embarrassment. Scores of candles were throwing a glittering light from reflecting Venetian chandeliers. Four men servants stood like soldiers ready for service. The major domo, in spotless uniform, waited by the door. The new master arrived with quick steps for the good reason that he was hungry. He wore a soft shirt, a pair of casual trousers and slippers but he had put on the coat of his formal evening uniform on which he had pinned many medals from the box of his uncle. Chequered like his uniform was his state of mind and his behaviour. He bowed low and formally to the girl, who responded with a deep curtsey. He gave her his arm and conducted her with grace to her seat, but remarked, while carefully moving her chair underneath her behind: 'You have a fine pair of breasts.'

During the first course, he studied her carefully, comparing her with his aunt, whom he had seen only a few times and being really uncertain whether it was his aunt or not, especially when he saw how well Grushenka handled fork and knife. She was afraid to make a move and hardly able to eat, but she was graceful by nature. He opened the conversation: 'May I inquire, my Princess,' said he, and not in a mocking tone, 'how you rested last night and how you feel today?'

Grushenka glanced at him and her full blue eyes had a begging expression. 'Forgive me your Highness,' she said, 'that I dare to eat in your presence and that I sit at your table, but your orders—' and she stopped. But he did not pay any attention to her words and went on in the same formal manner: 'Did my cherished Princess have a nice walk today and are you satisfied with all the service given to you? If there is anything you wish, please be good enough to tell me.'

'My only wish is to please my master,'was Grushenka's answer.

'Well now, you can do so,' he said. 'Tell me exactly the story of how you and Aunt Nelidowa put it over the old bugger. I haven't yet understood how it really happened. Of course you know the whole city is enjoying the story immensely. You see he's the meanest and shrewdest old swine there ever was and I ought to make a statue in honour of both you women. Hurrah!'—he concluded his little speech—'Let's drink to the health of Uncle Alexey.'

He lifted a glass of champagne toward her, drank it himself to the last drop and made her do the same. Grushenka, who had never before drunk a drop of wine or liquor soon began to feel happy and gay. Giggling she told him the whole story of the bed fraud until she came to the terrible end with its punishment. This she merely mentioned. Meanwhile they had a real Russian dinner from caviar to goose, from goose through roast beef to pies and fruits. They ate and drank constantly while the Prince asked the most intimate questions about the illustrious prick of his relative and the girl told him with utter frankness every detail of it. She knew no shame or reservation and her words were to the point.

When the meal was over he conducted her most formally to the drawing room. The conversation went on while they sat alone in the big room and it occurred to Leo for the first time, that he was now the master, that he could take everyone of these girls and handle her the way he saw fit. He learned of the way Nelidowa used to hit and pinch her girls, he heard of the torture chamber, of the rules of the house, of the gossip, of the

71

wishes of his male and female serfs and he began to understand their absolute submissiveness. Not that Prince Leo had not known all these things, but he had known them only from afar. Now they came clearly to his mind from the chattering talk of this, his slave girl who was a bit tipsy but not drunk.

She began to get drowsy; it was time to go to bed. Leo again conducted her on his arm, this time to the bed chamber of the Princess where the chamber maids still lingered, curious to hear from Grushenka how the evening had passed. Leo saw with pleasure all these young creatures of whom he could make good use from now on. Knowing they were his property, he did not bother about a close inspection. He had heard so much about his aunt and of the perfect bodily likeness between her and Grushenka, that he was curious to see with his own eyes what his aunt looked like. Therefore he sat down in a low chair in a corner and gave the order to the girls that Grushenka should play the part of Nelidowa and behave exactly as though she were the Princess going to bed. The girls were also to conduct themselves as usual.

The girls giggled and started the little show. They helped Grushenka out of the gown. Grushenka stood before the mirror. She made graceful movements with her arms, caressed her breasts lovingly, rubbed her pussy playfully with the palm of her hand and said cooingly, 'Oh, Gustavus! If I had you here now'—a remark which Nelidowa had made quite often to her own pussy and which usually was the sign for the serving girls that some sucking would be in store. Grushenka sat down. One girl kneeled before her and slowly removed her shoes and stockings. Another one took her wig off, loosened the long black hair and began to braid it. Grushenka meanwhile gave an account of the evening, an imaginary ball: finding herself the most beautiful woman present, telling about men who made longing eyes at her or others who seemed to have good balls in their trousers—all in the manner of Nelidowa. She even took the whip and lightly hit a servant girl over the legs, complaining she had handled her hair too roughly. Finally she got up from the chair, went to the middle of the room, and with feminine gestures, removed the little shirt she was wearing. Still rubbing her body voluptuously, she proceeded towards the bed.

Young Leo had been sitting motionless except for his big tool, which had lifted its head slowly. The half nude girl at the toilet table was good bait for Master Prick who sensed that a little hook up would not be amiss. He rose and stopped Grushenka; he looked her over closely and appraisingly. He let her turn around and as his eyes slid down over the beautiful back, he discovered the red marks on her bottom. This brought back to his mind that she was his property and subject to his bidding. He laid his hands on her, felt her all over and started to deliberate what to do with her.

His desire grew with every second. He pinched her cheeks and then opening her lips with two fingers he said, 'Well, this mouth has been used alternately by my stinking uncle and my cheating aunt. Now as much as I like to get sucked off, I would not put my prick where other people have had theirs. When I know somebody has had a girl before me, I will not fuck her. You may ask my comrades if that isn't so. Of course'—he added—'I have fucked many whores, and so far as I remember, never a virgin, but then if I don't know who had the bitches before me, it doesn't matter. Funny, isn't it?'

None of the girls in the room understood him, but many men are the same way. Yet he somewhat resented his own peculiarity, especially when he took her full bust in his hands and played with it. Of course he did not stop there. Soon his finger was in the slit and he was excited when the girl became responsive to his fingering and moved her arse around. In fact she put her arms around his neck and pressed herself to him, moving her thighs between his, and was gratified to feel his machine in proper condition. But just because she apparently wanted him, he cooled off and let her go with the crisp order, 'March to bed!' He did not want to fuck the bed companion of his uncle whom he detested. He would pick one of the hand maidens and have a good party.

Grushenka turned away from him and went to the bed and putting one knee on it was just about to slip underneath the sheets. His glance had followed her and became focused on her bare bottom. His testicles signalled an idea to his head.

'Stop!' he commanded. 'Kneel with both knees on the bed and bend forward.'

Grushenka did as bidden, fearfully wondering why she should be beaten now, which was what she expected. But she learned something else very soon. He came over to her, opened up the rim of her behind and fingering the arse hole asked her, 'Did my uncle use this way also?'—a question the girl denied with an astonished 'Oh, no, no!' She had never heard of such a thing.

Leo, however, had wanted just this thing for a long time. The cheap whores and little tarts he could afford had always refused that very thing, but some of his brother officers had bragged about it. Here was his opportunity. This arse was his. He could use it as he pleased.

'That's fine!' he exclaimed. 'There goes another virginity of yours. Hurrah, for arse-fucking!'

With that he opened his trousers and took his prick out, much to the satisfaction of his tool which had felt for the past few minutes eager to come out of its narrow jail of tight trousers; and much to the satisfaction of the onlooking maids, because he had a good big and long instrument. No doubt he would be the right master for their wet pussies—although they would be terrified to get pushed in the back entrance with such a big shaft. Some of them actually moved their hands over their behinds, as if protecting their rear passage. But Grushenka crouched on her hands and knees on the bed, like a dog, pressing her thighs together in a shiver. Leo came close to her, demanded that she lie down on her elbows. When she started to lie down flat on her belly, he lifted up her bottom and spread her knees apart, so that nothing should stop an easy access.

'One of you girls,' the young man ordered, and he was quite excited anticipating this erotic venture which was new to him—'One of you girls, put it in for me, but in the back hole, if you don't want to feel the whip.'

Grushenka felt a hand open up her rim and the point of the prick touch her arse hole. She held herself motionless, but contracted the muscles of her rear entrance involuntarily and when the Prince began to push he could not enter. He tried in

vain to gain an entrance and was answered by Grushenka
with little cries of pain. While it did not really hurt, she
anticipated that it would. The whole room became excited
with this arse rape and the watching girls were in a state of
tearful pity and sexual stimulation. Young Leo became
impatient.

'Wait a minute, your Highness,' said the girl who had tried
to put his prick into Grushenka's arse. 'I know how to do it.'

She arose quickly and got a jar of salve from the toilet table.
The Prince, looking down, saw her lovingly smear a white
ointment on his machine. Then he saw how the girl
annointed the little contracted hole of Grushenka all around
on the outside. Aftr that her finger began carefully to enter the
arse hole, going in and out, taking more salve to smooth the
way for the trip. The young fellow got awfully hot seeing the
arse of the girl get fingered before his eyes and hardly could
wait until his time came to shoot.

Grushenka had a curious sensation. While the feeling of
the finger playing in her arse hole was not particularly
agreeable, she felt at the same time the sensation of getting
hot in her love nest and because nobody else caressed her
hungry little clitoris, she brought her own finger to the spot
and pressed the rhythm of a melody to it, while the flesh of her
loins and her thighs trembled with a thrill. This curious
feeling was subdued very qickly by an unpleasant pain.
Something very big moved into her arse and filled her insides
completely. Because of the salve, the hard, long shaft entered
her without any resistance to speak of.

The man was fucking her in the arse, pushing with mighty
strokes, not considering her reactions, just pushing and
pushing. His hands grasped her strongly about the hips, they
pulled her bottom towards his thighs leaving her free only to
swing out for a new push. With the boiling heat in his loins,
he forgot himself more and more. The standing position
became uncomfortable, it was too much of a strain on his
legs. He threw the whole weight of his body on her, flattened
her out on her stomach and lay on her back, squeezing her full
breasts. Her feet and her head were in the air over the sides of
the bed. He was working on her furiously and the pressure in

her arse hole became awful. The buttons of his uniform and the medals scratched the skin off her back; her head was swimming. She started to fuck with her bottom against him, giving him response as well as she could, not because she felt wanton, but to make him come more quickly.

She succeeded finally. He shot with might, flooding her insides and groaning. After that he lay still, wondering whether he had made a fool of himself. But when he slipped his tool out of its warm embrace and turned around, he found one of the girls ready with a bowl of water with which she cleaned him devotedly. He realized he was the master and could use these girls according to his moods. Tired and lazy, but smiling with satisfaction, he gathered himself together and got off the bed. He gave Grushenka a good slap on her bare bottom and retired to his room with the remark, 'You aren't such a bad arse after all.'

The girls now started to wipe Grushenka's bottom clean, while they discussed the event. So that was the way they were going to be taken! They uneasily rubbed their behinds, feeling frightened and excited, because the passion in the Prince's loins had left an impression on their minds. Grushenka stretched herself on the bed of the Princess and turned around to try to sleep. She felt sore and empty and did not want to hear a word.

During the next few days of getting acquainted with his duties, the Prince decided the question of the females in his household. The former bed-fellows of the old Prince were sent away to the different estates from which they came. They had been his uncle's private prick massaging machines and Leo detested the old man so much that he had no desire to be his successor in this respect. The personal maids of the Princess were commanded to constitute his personal harem. He had seen that evening that they were all hand picked. He resolved to try them out one after the other, to keep whom he liked and to replace the rest.

The next evening he sent his orderly to bring one of them to his bed. This sturdy Cossack went into the room where the girls were sleeping and tapped the first one on the shoulder. Naked as she was, she followed him, and thinking uneasily of her arse, she took with her the white salve which she picked up while crossing the bedroom of her former mistress. She was a big blonde whose flesh had excited Nelidowa to many a good pinch. Her arms, legs, even her belly still had some blue and green spots on them. She crept docilely into the bed and started to fondle and kiss Leo. He fingered her pussy and found it good and large. But in spite of that she was healthy, fresh, laughing and eager and he liked her. He got on top of her and gave her an amazingly good poke right in the cunt. This delighted her immensely and she gave herself to him whole heartedly. They repeated this procedure a number of times and it must be said that the young Prince never again fucked a girl in the arse.

The girls were most happy about it and discussed it at great length. As he did not take a special fancy to any one of them he had a group of most ambitious bed-fellows competing for his favour. They liked him and all spoke well of him, because he was a nice chap and kept them well satisfied. The only other thing worth mentioning was that he could not pass any young and good looking woman without stopping to give her a good feeling, especially to make the acquaintance of her cunt. But this little habit is understandable as for so many years he had had to restrain this natural impulse that now he could hardly be blamed for his self indulgence.

Grushenka had been one of Nelidowa's hand-maids and was therefore now assigned to the Prince's personal staff. There she remained for over six months. He never touched her again or spoke with her again. She tried several times to induce him to take notice of her, once even went into his bed room claiming he had sent for her. But he would have none of her.

It was of more importance that Grushenka, during this period of idleness, began to learn to read and write. Serfs were not permitted this privilege and for that very reason they made it their business, whenever they could, to learn their 'A-B-Cs.' Grushenka soon could read simple stories. In fact, she—and with her the other girls—got their first contact with the outer world by stealing from Prince Leo the current gazettes and magazines which were delivered to him.

CHAPTER VIII.

The hot summer days had gone by. The huge oak and maple trees on the lawn of the Sokolow country estate turned from deep green to yellow. Autumn was approaching and with the whole household would return to Moscow.

Every year at that time, Madame Sophia Schukow made her appearance. She came in her own small coach with two horses, followed by a big rented carriage with four horses and nobody in it. This carriage was to be filled. Madame Sophia was buying girls from all over the country for her famous establishment in Moscow. This year she needed at least six new girls and her stop was at Sokolow's where she could hope to pick up the majority of them.

The business of renting out serf girls to whore houses had become so prevalent that a few special laws existed about it. For example: what was to be done if one of the girls became syphilitic? She was not suitable at that time and she was of no use to her owner or to the whore house. Therefore the law provided that she was to be sent to Siberia, the cost to be divided by the owner and the Madame. Or what price was to be paid when a girl should run away? The girls were not sold, but rented out; quarterly instalments had to be sent to the owner, ranging from five to thirty rubles and after a year or two, the girl had to be returned.

Madame Sophia was a thin, agile person with a never-ending flow of words. She talked so much that customers of her house quickly made their choice of the girl they wanted in order to get away from her. She was very elegant, treated her girls with candied words and most brutal beatings and was very successful in her trade.

Sophia's visit to the summer palace was of special concern to Katerina, for whom she brought many little gifts, from

French candies to Viennese stays, and whom she did not leave for a minute during her stay. Katerina looked forward to these visits because Sophia told the gossip about the fine men of Moscow, men whom she watched during their intercourse with her girls, and knew more about than their own wives. During the eating hours Sophia looked over the crop of serf girls at the palace. She did not make her choice quickly. She picked her prey with sharp eyes and watched for a few days before the bargaining began. Katerina was not easily persuaded to let a girl go, but in the end she always succumbed to Sophia's clever tongue.

There were three girls Sophia wanted. Then by accident, she met Grushenka. She had not seen her before because the bed-fellows of the Prince had their own quarters and their own meals. Sophia made up her mind that, cost what it might, she was going to get Grushenka, even if she should have to go on her knees before the young Prince, who was taken up by hunting parties, riding, and cursing his farmer serfs. She broached the subject to Katerina and was astonished to find no resistance. Katerina knew very well that the Prince made no use of Grushenka and Grushenka was a sore spot on Katerina's mind. It was on her account that the old and rightful owner of the estate was now away from the holy ground of Russia and that this young ne'er-do-well, his nephew, was in charge. She therefore promised her help and took the matter up with Prince Leo, who after a moment's thought consented. When his uncle came back it might be an unpleasant reminder to find the substitute of his former wife still there. While he did not know whether it would be wise to sell Grushenka outright, to rent her to a whore house for a couple of years was a very good way out.

Hence Grushenka was looked over by Sophia, who indulged in a stream of praise about her beauty and who secretly congratulated herself on her find. What a tid-bit for her customers, to be told that they could fuck a girl who had played the part of the Princess Sokolow! Before Grushenka knew what it was all about she was sitting in the large carriage with three other girls, being driven drowsily over rough country roads leading apparently nowhere.

After many night stops the four girls were put up in a public house, a station where express horses were changed, while Sophia went for a few days to a nearby estate to do more of her shopping. The girls were in the charge of the big coachman, a drunken and brazen fellow who was told to exercise his whip on them in case they should not behave. That they might try to run away did not occur to Sophia, who had told them a thousand alluring stories of the wonderful gowns they were to wear, of the many rich lovers they were going to have, of the food served on silver platters and so on.

The other girls believed her and praised their luck that they could get away from the hard work in the household and be 'Ladies' on their own. Not so Grushenka. She knew what was coming, she had heard enough stories of girls who had been mistreated in whore houses, of sickness and abuse. The moral element of the matter did not enter her mind. To her it was perfectly right that her owner should use her body to gain money. But having had it easy in Sokolow's house, she nourished the idea of making a get-away. Of course she knew that if she was caught the hot branding iron would be the least of her punishments, yet she could not help thinking and planning.

The girls stayed two or three days in the public house; sleeping in the mornings as long as they wanted, taking walks over the fields, sitting about in the one big guest room which the place offered for travellers. All kinds of people passed through the road-house. Farmers driving their cattle, officials in express coaches, tradesmen and monks. The girls looked at them with lazy eyes; they were not interested in getting acquainted with them or having affairs with them; soon there would be a stream of pricks to be satisfied, to be caressed.

One night, Sophia having not yet returned, a fine carriage drove into the yard. Two youngish aristocratic men sat in the cushions. They did not leave the carriage, but admonished the coachman to change the horses quickly because they wanted to reach another road-house that night. Grushenka lingered around the yard, avoiding the heavy atmosphere of the crowded guest room. She walked slowly over to the carriage. Her face and figure, not clearly visible in the twilight and the light from the coach lanterns, intrigued one of the men, the smaller of the two.

'Will the young lady' he said to her, 'charm two hurried travellers with a friendly good evening?' and he tipped his hat in a respectful manner. He was not sure who Grushenka might be. She had a fine dress on, one of Nelidowa's travelling dresses, which Katerina had given her because she had no use for Nelidowa's things anymore, and she had a fine bearing and presence. But why should an aristocratic girl stay in such a second rate road-house over night? That was usually not done. Grushenka went leisurely to the coach, leaned over the low door and slowly looked the men over.

The smaller fellow spoke again, this time more enthusiastically because of the girl's beauty. 'If we can do anything for you, my Lady, let your word be a command. Be sure that my friend and I will do anything we can for such a lovely Lady as you are.' He gave his friend a slight poke in the side, indicating that he should help along the same line. But this young man was absorbed in his own thoughts.

He had not paid much attention to the girl and seemed a bit annoyed that his companion was trying to sail into an adventure. He was dressed, like his friend, in a wide travelling cloak. His white neck cloth of fine silk shone in the flickering light of the yard. He had a most distinguished face, bold blue eyes, an aristocratic nose and a clean cut, full mouth, sensual but displaying the force of self restraint. He hardly glanced toward Grushenka; his eyes eagerly followed the doings of his coachman and of the stable men. He looked like a conspirator who wants to reach the place of action on time. Grushenka liked him a t first sight. In fact, she felt so attracted to him that she resented his passivity towards her. But the eagerness of his companion spun the conversation one step further.

'I cannot imagine, Mademoiselle, that you would stay here over night by your own wish, when twenty verst from here is the famous X........... Inn, where all comfort is rendered to travellers. Has your carriage broken down, or is there any other reason why you cannot move on?'

Grushenka rested her eyes fully on the speaker. If he would give her a lift she would be in Moscow before that fool of a coachman would have notified Madame Sophia and by that time she was quite sure no attempt would be made to follow her. The little fellow, aware of her deliberations, continued his efforts. 'We certainly would be delighted to take you along to Moscow, or even to Petersburg, where too we are going, if you ...' and he stopped.

Grushenka decided her fate. She would do it! Run away! She leaned into the carriage and whispered, 'You see that big oak tree down the road?' I will wait there for you. If your carriage stops, I shall be glad to accept your invitation and you won't be sorry—' she added with a faint smile. After that she went to the appointed place with quick steps, without looking back. She was very excited. Would they pick her up, or not?

The handsome man turned to his smaller companion and reminded him that they were in a hurry and not interested in girls at that moment. The other one retorted that there was never a time that one should not pay attention to the weaker sex and when they came to the oak tree, the coachman stopped. Grushenka slipped in. She was seated between the men on the broad back seat of the carriage. The little fellow very formally began the introduction. 'My name is Fladilow Szerementon,' he said. 'This is Mihail Stieven. We travel on a government commission of which we won't speak. We're bound for Petersburg, as I said before.'

Grushenka nodded and was satisfied that this time Mihail took full notice of her, making a little bow and trying to distinguish her features in the soft moonlight. She answered, 'I also am on a trip whose object I won't mention. I'm on my way to Moscow and am very grateful that you gentlemen can take me along. You will permit me not to give you my right name. Call me Mary, which is one of my names. I cannot expect that you take me to Moscow for nothing and I will do right by both of you, if you so desire. In fact I have to ask you to pay for my lodging at the Inn and it will be cheaper for you if I share a room with you. You will ask me why I am so outspoken in all this,' she added and turned to Mihail. 'But I see your thoughts are far away and I will spare you the trouble of finding out all about me and of courting me. I am easy and willing.' She took a hand of each of her travelling companions and leaned full back in the seat giving both a warm pressure with the sides of her body.

'You have very fine hands, anyway,' said Mihail, taken by surprise by this unusual little oration. 'You certainly are not a girl used to work. We will not pry into your secrets and will see to your comfort—although I am annoyed with that little man on your other side, who can never let the women alone. Beware of him!' he added with a smile.

'Then to our good friendship.' answered the girl. She turned lightly around to Fladilow and gave him a little kiss. This done, she turned to Mihail, put her hand behind his head and as well as the swaggering coach would permit, she kissed him on the lips.

During this kiss something happened which once in a while does take place. Grushenka fell violently in love with Mihail. It went through her body like an electric shock. She looked at him with glaring eyes, she could not help feeling his body, she caressed his face, she pressed herself towards him, she was so attracted by him that she travelled along the road in a trance. She felt light and happy as though suddenly cured after a great illness. She behaved like a young girl who has been, against her will, very virtuous for many months and is suddenly close to a man who electrifies her.

She forced Mihail to put his arms around her, she leaned her head on his chest, she looked longingly at the moon. She had her hands on his thighs, but did not dare to come near his prick, which she felt was not averse to the young woman making love to him. At the same time she did not forget the other companion whose good graces had put her in this position and who had to be taken into the bargain. Her free hand, therefore, was in his lap, playing with his shaft which became slowly but surely alert.

Grushenka remembered this poetic drive through the moonlight her whole life. Her first love, her first adventure, something she had done of her own free will. The softness of the drowsy waggling of the coach, the giggling of her enamoured mind, the stillness of the wide country! Mihail was pleased but still a bit suspicious as to where this adventure with a mysterious girl would lead. Fladilow was also satisfied, for even though a good poke might not be in store for him, he at least had fixed it up for his friend and superior and that would be a feather in his cap.

The lights of the inn came in sight. They had arrived for their night's rest. Mihail took a big private room, ordered the deeply bowing inn keeper to serve a hearty meal, and Fladilow, seeing that Grushenka was taken up so much with his boss, asked the Inn keeper whether he could not send another girl as a fourth guest to the repast. The inn keeper, with a twinkle in his eye, swore that he had a most beautiful girl at hand for the comfort of his guests and that he would send her right to them.

The light of the flickering candles shone over the mixed company: the young and aristocratic men in shirt sleeves, hungry, dusty and behaving most informally, as two young fellows will do when they are not in the company of ladies; the wayside whore, rustic, healthy and plump, eager to get as much money out of her prey as possible, and Grushenka, in the stylish dress of a Lady acting refined and using every opportunity to please Mihail towards whom she shot ardent glances. Both men were most attentive to her, treating the little whore scantily and the latter could not make out what it was all about. She got really jealous of Grushenka, who seemed to take both men away from her and whom she could not classify. She tried her best to get the men for herself. Under ordinary circumstances Grushenka probably would have kept still and would have let things take their course but in her happy mood of being out of her serfdom, at least for the moment, and being near to the man who seemed the dream lover of her past years, she developed a cheeriness which led to a silent battle between the two females.

Meanwhile the men ate with hearty appetite and Fladilow encouraged Grushenka whenever he saw an opportunity. Not so Mihail, especially not after the dinner, when Grushenka sat down on his lap and started to smother him with kisses. She took possession of him and although he was enchanted by her charms, he felt that she became too 'sticky,' too close to him. Before the real love-making between them started, he was already wondering how he could get rid of her with grace. Fladilow loitered around the room, kept the country vixen at her distance and took another room next to the one they were in, where he intended to have a quick party with the little whore in order to fall easily to sleep. They had a long trip ahead of them the next morning and it was getting late.

But his eyes were longing for Grushenka and the little whore did not miss that. Feeling that she could not triumph mentally over her rival, she tried physically. Without a word she took her blouse off and slipped the ribbons of her shirt over her shoulders. Turning towards both men, she displayed two big and well made breasts with full red nipples. 'Here,' she said, 'that's the reason why men call me in and why no traveller passing this inn forgets to send for me. Let that bloodless young woman (pointing to Grushenka) show what she has to say to that! I bet her poor cushions fall down to her belly, or she would not hide them so carefully,' and she swung herself proudly from her hips. Fladilow got angry and was about to scold the girl for this sudden aggression against Grushenka when Mihail intervened in a way which Fladilow did not understand.

'Well,' he said quietly to Grushenka, who was most intimately ruffling his hair, 'Well, my dear, what do you say to this challenge?'

Grushenka looked for a moment questioningly into his eyes. She rose from his lap. With quiet motions she took her clothes off, all of them, as if her old mistress had given her the order. She crossed her hands behind her neck and stood before the men in devoted dignity. There was not a lascivious motion or thought in her and the raptuous beauty of her body made the men stare in adoration. All four were silent until the whore broke out in an angry speech.

'Look at that fuck hole of hers!' she cried. 'I bet many hundred men—' But she could not finish the sentence. Fladilow rushed up to her and closed her mouth with a rude push of his hand. 'Get out of here!' he shouted at her. 'Get out and stay out.' And with that he threw her bodily out of the door, half nude as she was. He flung her blouse and other belongings after her and topped it with a silver ruble, which she caught with alertness while her scornful words bellowed through the hall way. Fladilow grinned with delight. He always liked cursing whores.

He re-entered the room. He bade the two, 'Good night and a good time' and his longing eyes were fixed on Grushenka, who had meanwhile ascended the big bed. 'It was a bargain for both of us,' said Mihail. 'This young lady is coming to see you very soon, I assure you. Don't fall asleep too quickly.'

What was in Mihail's mind was that by dividing the young girl between his friend and himself, he was getting rid of all obligations and there would be no fear that this creature should have any claims on him. He went leisurely to bed, tinkering around with his port-manteau, washing and showing that he was in no hurry whatsoever. Meanwhile Grushenka lay in bed with closed eyes, telling herself the most ardent love words she knew, but not moving her lips. It is not impossible that she mixed silent prayers with her longings for him.

Mihail came to bed finally. He laid himself next to her, put his arms around her and seemed to express with his movements, 'All right, now let's have it.' He expected that she would kiss and fondle him, he would not have been surprised if she had manhandled him. The contrary was the case. She hardly stirred. Of course she rested close to him, touching his body with hers, but nothing more than that. He turned towards her, he rubbed his shaft against her flesh and became stiff, which was natural for a young fellow with such a beautiful creature at his side. He mounted her and he worked away on her. She pressed him in her arms, close—so close. She encircled him with her legs, raised her thighs so high that her heels pressed tightly on his bottom.

But she did not respond to his lovemaking. She was as if in a trance, unable to move, overcome in a passive rapture—but he did not know anything about that. She did not give him any pleasure and he was disappointed and came. What a silly girl! First to act like a lovelorn cat and then, when it came to the point, a creature without any feelings. Well, Fladilow should at least

86

see for himself what a poor bed-fellow he had picked up on the roadside. When Mihail was through, he told her in decisive words to take care of his friend. She got up like a sleep-walker. She stopped in a corner of the room over a night pot, washed her pussy, peed a little, and disappeared into Fladlow's room.

Fladilow was eager to explain to her that since she loved his friend, he was too much of a gentleman to touch her unless she wanted it, but she read between the lines that he was quite hungry for her. Grushenka wanted to talk with Fladilow about his friend, she wanted to know everything about him, but there was still too much of the serf in her to let her thoughts get into her mouth. She was ordered to relieve the young fellow of his passion and she proceeded to do so. She remembered how she had done this with Prince Sokolow and she did her job in the same fashion.

Without much ado she pulled the sheets away from him, bent over him and began to caress, then to suck his prick. He lay still on his back, moving his behind now and then until he became very excited. She then mounted him, inserted his member with apt fingers into her pussy and started an expert ride on top of him. In fact she herself now became hot. Her loins quivered, she bent over to feel his hands on her globes, she expertly contracted her hole, sucking his shaft with her cunt to the best of her ability. Thus she gave him one of those extraordinary good fucks which the old man Sokolow had so admired. When she felt that he came, she bit him on the shoulder and panting with passion, let herself come to the climax just as he was spending. But she lay only for a few minutes on his chest, then left him with a gracious and silent movement of her slender body.

'What a creature! What a wonderful fuck—' thought Fladilow before he fell asleep. What great praise he would get from his friend the next day! And Morpheus visited a very satisfied young man a few minutes later.

Mihail was already asleep when Grushenka returned. She hardly dared to go back into the bed alongside of him. But he did not wake up, he did not stir. Sleep was far away from Grushenka's eyes. She lay awake, glaring through the darkness of the room at the man next to her, at her beloved, the one and only. She did not cry because fate would take him away from her the next day, she just prayed for him, she was ready to give her life for him, she adored him and she was happy until the early morning hours closed her eyes for a short rest.

It was a grey morning of drizzling rain and they were three tired and moody travellers. They spoke very little. The horses made haste to reach the next stable while the coachman uttered faint curses and did not bother to wipe the raindrops from his wet face. They ate hurried meals by the wayside and the spirit of adventure and sentiment of the previous night was forgotten.

When Grushenka left them for a moment in an inn, Fladilow wanted to collect the laurels for the night before. Winking with his eyes after the disappearing girl, he commented on her unusual love making qualities. He was suprised at the answer he received and could no more understand his friend than the other one could get the meaning of his words. 'Lousy!' remarked Mihail. 'Just Lousy! Take a piece of timber and screw a hole in it and you'd get a better reaction. Isn't it so?' Which left them both puzzled, especially when Fladilow swore that since that Swedish girl in Stockholm, of whom he had spoken so often before to his friend, since her, he had not had such a wonderful time, except with Grushenka. To which Mihail just answered, 'Pooh!' and the matter was dropped.

The sleepless night, the sure separation from her idol, probably forever, the uncertainty of her future, made Grushenka sad and monosyllabic. They reached the towers of Moscow after dark, passing the gates without molestation after Mihail had presented his pass. The clattering and rumbling coach entered the ill lit streets of the poor quarters. Grushenka begged to be permitted to take leave. The men wondered what this well dressed beauty might want in this squalid section of the city but they stopped the carriage assuring her that if they could do anything for her at any time they were at her service.

It was Mihail who got out of the coach first and helped her descend, quite politely now, because he was satisfied that she could not be a future impediment to him. Grushenka bowed low over his hand and kissed it. He drew his hand back, as if an iron had burnt it. He kissed the girl on both cheeks and felt a sudden attachment to this mysterious beauty. Grushenka clasped Fladilow's hand with a hearty shake and before they finally parted she felt Mihail press something into her hand. 'Password to the gates of heaven and hell!' he cried, merrily—and the coach drove on at a quick pace.

Grushenka stood on the pavement. It was dark all around. She was alone, very alone. In her hand were a few gold pieces. When she discovered them she started to cry softly. He had paid her! What a shame! What a disgrace! But she did not follow her first impulse to throw the money into the muddy street, no, with a second thought she clasped it securely in her hand. It would be a life saver, a life saver.

She collected her senses. If she was caught here in the street by a gendarme or by the watchman who cried out the hours during his rounds, she would be brought to the next police station and the game would be up. A night prowler on the streets would not be left alone unless he had a pass from his master or a very clear excuse. She knew the neighbourhood well enough and started a hasty run along the houses, keeping in the shadow, through gardens and side streets, until she came to an old and dilapidated two storey house. The big front door was closed and she did not bother to ring the bell or call for the janitor. She moved around the building to a back entrance which was open and ascended a creaking wooden stair, dimly lit by small oil lamps. On the top floor she stopped and knocked on one of the many doors which were around this landing. First she knocked faintly, then more boldly with great fear in her heart that her only girl friend Martha might not live here any more. She had not seen her since she had gone to the Sokolows, in fact had never had the opportunity to tell her about her change in life. What would happen to her now if she could not find shelter with Martha?

Finally there was a faint rustle inside and a terrified small voice asked who was outside. 'Grushenka,' answered the girl, her heart leaping with joy. 'Grushenka, you little dove!' ... and soon the girls lay in each others arms, kissing each other's cheeks and crying on each other's breast to celebrate their having found each other again.

CHAPTER IX.

Martha's history can be told very briefly, a story of which there are so many similar ones. Born out of wedlock of a mother who was a rich and independent farmer's daughter who had been driven from home when she was heavy with child, Martha had been given in servitude to a modiste. This modiste, Mademoiselle Laura Cameron, kept a fashionable hat and gown store in one of the few elegant thoroughfares of Moscow. Martha was not yet 14 years of age when she became a servant of this sweet, lisping but keenly selfish woman who exercised parental rights over the little girl and abused her with hard work and harsh treatment. In exchange she paid her small wages which Martha had to deliver to her mother who received the money by making her signature on a slip of paper. This signature consisted of three crosses, because mother and daughter could not read or write.

Martha's mother refused some offers to sell the girl as a serf. She had taken a room in the poorer quarters and done such odd jobs as a woman could find, barely enough to keep them alive. Worried and exhausted by hardship she had finally consented to die, leaving her little girl to shift alone.

Martha did not dare to tell this to her employer, because she feared that she would make a real serf out of her right away, taking her into her house where she kept a few girls already. She received the small wages and signed with the crosses as if her mother was still alive. This and many more things she told to Grushenka, who in turn related her story. Of course this all took several days, or rather nights, because Martha went to her work early and came home at sunset. Meanwhile Grushenka stayed in the poor room, sleeping in the big bed and not going out for fear she should be picked up by the police or by the searchers of Sophia. However, with the gold pieces which Mihail had left in Grushenka's little hand, they had a wonderful time together, eating and drinking what money could buy.

But it was apparent that this could not go on forever, so they decided that Martha should tell her mistress that a cousin of hers had arrived in the city and desired to enter her services. Moved by Martha's raving description, Madame Laura consented to take a look at Grushenka and thus they went one fine morning to the store of this commanding lady. Martha had bought Grushenka some clothes such as a farm girl might wear when she came to the city; a multi-coloured blouse, a pleated skirt, a kerchief to be wound around the head, all very becoming to Grushenka, who much to her advantage, displayed the tan on her cheeks which the country life on Sokolow's estate had left there.

Martha, stout and stocky, with a round good hearted face, certainly not pretty, but young and unspoiled, hesitated several times on the way. Of course she had given her girlfriend a description of Madame Laura and her establishment and of course Grushenka had seen hard treatment in her almost twenty years of serfdom and did not expect to be treated with kid gloves. But had not Martha given too good an account of that which would be in store for Grushenka? To ease her mind she told Grushenka frankly that she had suppressed many unpleasant features which the work for Madame Laura would carry with it. Grushenka, however, had decided to go through with it. What could she do? There were no labour markets where jobs could be found. Labour was conducted by the members of a family in small enterprises; the bigger ones bought serfs. Some trades requiring craftmanship such as carpentry or pottery, hired workers but only through their own guilds. Furthermore, if Grushenka should really have the luck to be hired by Madame Laura, could not she and Martha live together and continue those heavenly nights, during which Grushenka could rave about her Mihail? Work and mistreatment? Was Grushenka not used to that since early childhood?

Martha made the sign of the cross and they entered

Madame Laura's. Through a gilded door covered with fresh garlands of flowers they came into a huge sales room with low ceiling and elegant furniture. Grushenka's eye, trained through her work as clothes horse for the Princess, detected with pleasure the trick array of woman's styles, expensive materials, good craftmanship—this must be a store for the very rich! Crossing the room, they entered the second salesroom consisting of a small hallway which parted half a dozen private rooms equipped with huge mirrors, easy chairs and couches. Of course there were no customers at this early morning hour but a few attractive girls were busy cleaning and dusting. The third room on the ground floor was Madame's sumptuously furnished private office.

Madame Laura was not yet in, in fact she would not come before noon and Grushenka went with Martha to the sewing room on the next floor. Fifteen or more girls already sat to their work, sewing, cutting and trying on the hats, gowns, dresses and underwear created under the supervision of two elderly expert modistes. Martha joined the workers while Grushenka sat modestly on a chair and watched, eager to do this kind of work so pleasing to her female instinct for beautifying. At last one of the girls came from down stairs notifying Martha and Grushenka that they were wanted by the mistress.

Madame Laura received the girls with her sweetest smile, complimenting them on being two such lovely cousins. She scrutinized Grushenka with sharp eyes, asking her whether she had learned sewing with 'her dear mother' and asking many questions about her and Martha's home village, but not waiting for any answers. Everything seemed to go well as the girls shamefully stuttered a few words but did not dare to glance at each other. But Madame Laura's keen sense of people, which had brought her her clientele and fortune, suspected that something was wrong. For example, where did this girl, supposed to come from the country, get those silk stockings and those shoes? Then she detected the well manicured and soft hands which surely were not those of a tramp from a village.

Madame Laura moved around to her desk chair of rosewood with brass heads on the arms. She had Martha close the door and put Grushenka in the full light opposite herself. She concentrated her attention all the more on this newcomer because the girl seemed to be unusually well made, obliging, and certainly a business propostion if rightly developed. She wanted to see more of her and demanded that Grushenka take her kerchief and blouse off, under the pretext of finding out whether she might be suitable as a model. Grushenka did as she was told without hesitation, thus adding a new proof that she was not a dumb country girl. In fact Grushenka discarded her skirt and drawers also and Madame Laura had difficulty in suppressing her wholesome admiration: a perfect shape, straight legs, soft but firm flesh, a morsel for the appetite of the most refined taste of any man.

Madame Laura was a connoisseur. Procuring was her most important magnet for securing a clientele and she made ample use of it. Who was this girl? Of a sudden she changed her tactics, the smile faded, and Martha was in for it! First Madame Laura asked her sharply to tell the truth. But fat little Martha stuck to her story, stuck to it even when Madame Laura's hand, manipulated on Martha's behind, caused her to emit many 'Oh's and 'Ah's. In Madame Laura's hand was a long needle which Grushenka detected as she stood helplessly aside in her nakedness.

After that, Madame Laura began to use stronger means: she opened Martha's blouse, took the girl's left breast from underneath the shirt and squeezing the breast firmly, pointed the needle directly at the nipple. Both girls watched the point of the needle anxiously and as Martha still held to her story, the sharp steel was pricked slowly into her flesh. Martha tried to suppress a howl as a big drop of blood ran slowly down over the milk white globe, but clung doggedly to her former assertion. Her face was twisted, tears streamed down her cheeks, but she did not dare to tear herself loose and run away. Impatiently Laura rose, took a short leather whip from her desk and demanded that the girl bend over. She tore her drawers down and as Martha's fat behind lay bare, demanded that she tell the truth or be whipped until her flesh was cut to the bone.

Before Madame Laura could lay the first smarting blow on the wide target, Grushenka threw herself between her and Martha, exclaiming that she would tell the truth, because she could not watch her friend suffer on her behalf. She then related her whole story to the silently listening Madame Laura, who knew that now she learned the true facts. Here was business for her! But she did not say a word of what was on her mind when Grushenka finally fell at her feet and threw herself at her mercy, imploring her to take her into her services. Instead Madame Laura behaved like a fury and answered that it was an outrage that this run-away slave girl wanted to make her a partner in her crime, reminding her that any person giving shelter or food to a run-away serf was liable to be sent to Siberia.

Martha, who had tried to stop Grushenka and had implored her to let her have her punishment, had to be dealt with first. Madame Laura, who did not want to impair the working value of the girl, gave her six lusty strokes on the bare bottom and sent her away. Martha kissed the hem of her mistress's gown and went weeping back to her work, sending a last pitiful glance at Grushenka who lay sullenly on the floor. Madame Laura speedily got her up, though not without letting her have some lashes from the biting whip. She then led her to one of the empty dressing rooms, locking it resolutely from the outside. While Grushenka, helplessly crying, nude, awaited an uncertain fate getween the four partitions of the small dressing room, Madame Laura wrote with her own hand a falsified billet-doux which she sent away with one of her delivery girls.

As the hours passed, Grushenka stopped crying, having given in to her fate. Probably she would be branded now. They would brand her on the forehead if they sent her away to Siberia, but if Sophia decided to take her into the whorehouse she would have her branded between the legs or on the shoulder blade so as not to mark her face. They would lash her, put her on the rack, maybe break her bones ... she must wait. She had done wrong. She should not have run away.

94

She lay motionless on the couch. She heard through the thin partition that the establishment of Madame Laura had become lively. Deprived of her clothes, she got slowly up from the couch and started to move around in the small dark room. Some light filtered in through cracks in the walls, which she soon found to come from the booths which adjoined hers. She peeked through the crevices and discovered that she had a view into the dressing rooms on either side. With the fear of her own fate in her heart, she began watching the happenings alongside of her.

In the booth on her right side sat an elderly gentleman, very correctly dressed in a long black coat, playing with his three cornered hat. Apparently, he waited for something. The rings on his fingers glittered with precious stones.

Grushenka turned to the other wall. A stony old woman sat in an easy chair. She was dressed in flashy colours; laces, ribbons and feathers hanging all around her as if she were a young chicken. She supported herself with an oak staff, but despite her old age and her crazy dress, her bearing was impressive and commanding. Next to her sat a nondescript woman companion, while Madame Laura and one of her models tried to sell her a hat. A pile of lovely hat creations lay on the couch and on the chairs. The model and Madame took new ones from white and cream-coloured boxes and described their beauty with sweet smiles and sentimental words, but the customer would not be satisfied. As a matter of fact, the old hawk rejected the idea of buying with the outspoken words which one would have expected in the mouth of an army sergeant. Madame, in turn, poked the model in the ribs and in the back, and although the girl preserved her frozen smile, there was no doubt that Madame's finger held a needle which drove her saleslady to every possible effort to make the old lady buy. No such luck! She got up, remarking that nothing charming enough could be found to adorn her old wrinkled face, and shuffled out of the room. After Madame had bowed her out, she turned around and hit the model soundly in the face, leaving her to repack the expensive hats. The girl was accustomed to such happenings. She wiped her face with the back of her

95

hand and went slowly but dutifully on with her work.

Grushenka turned back to the peep hole in the other wall and as she expected, found Madame and the gentleman in animated conversation. It seemed that the gentleman had just paid a bill to Madame, probably for clothes his wife had ordered and still had something on his mind. Madame knew very well what it was, but made a little play so as not to recognize his wishes too quickly. The gentleman, leaning from one foot to the other and stroking his moustache, finally said that he would like to see some styles, if Madame had a few models who could show him her newest creations. Madame smilingly asked whether he wanted to see the same models as the last time and whether it was not a good idea to show him her new line of underwear. The gentleman hastened to answer that the models the other day had been very lovely indeed, but that he would not mind seeing some others—all very lovely and very obliging, he was sure, if they worked for the famous Madame Laura—and that underwear was quite to his liking. Madame responded that she would show him a few models, that he should act as Paris did with the Greek Goddesses but—and Madame looked down at her hands which played with a few gold pieces. The gentleman smiled, assured her that the delicacy with which she handled the matter could not be surpassed by the most refined French woman, a compliment which Madame ate up eagerly, and he slipped her some gold rubles.

Madame Laura left him to get her girls. The gentleman took off his long formal coat displaying a waistcoat with silver buckles matching exactly his shoe buckles. No doubt this was a dandy. His white wig with pigtail was immaculate, his black breeches and stockings of finest silk. He sat down on the couch and loosened up the button of his trousers, underneath his waistcoat, with the beaming face of a man who knows that he will be taken care of.

Presently Madame came back leading a flock of her models, good-looking girls with all kinds of figures, from the tiny blonde to the statuesque brunette. The girls wore all types of underwear but were uniform in one respect: they wore no stays, but small bodices, which hardly covered the lower half of their breasts and left the nipples free. They had on embroidered shirts and long lace trousers, reaching to the ankles. While they walked around in a circle, through the open slits of their pantaloons one could get a glimpse of blonde, brown, or dark hair, an effect arranged that way by Madame, who understood showmanship.

The girls hardly looked in the direction of the man; they did not want to attract his attention because they knew that he would pick out one of them for his purposes. He had them go around a few times, smacking his lips and looking them over carefully. At last he pointed at two of them, both of them small girls without very good figures, at least in the judgement of the watching Grushenka. Madame dismissed the other girls, who left the room with an expression of relief, and taking the two who remained into a corner, she whispered a harsh command. The girls looked at her anxiously but seemed unmoved by what she said to them. Turning to the gentleman Madame Laura remarked that he had chosen two very obliging girls but should he have any complaint, she had a well-working leather whip which would change the mind of any stubborn little brat. Then with a majestic nod, she left him.

The girls sat down on the couch on each side of him, put their arms around him and cuddled themselves against him with a faint 'Hello, uncle.' He in turn put his arms around their backs, grabbed their breasts and was pleased with their behaviour. 'Now girls,' he started, 'first of all close the slit of your trousers and don't let that nasty hair peek out there. Sure, I believe that you have little pissholes down there, but who wants to get busy with such dirty little places?'

The girls lapped over the sides of their drawers, closing the openings, and continued their dalliance. Cuddling him, one of the girl's hands passed the front of his trousers and he took hold of it and indicated that it was to open up his breeches. Fumbling around with the buttons, the girls opened up the breeches and took his instrument out. It did not look too enticing to Grushenka. It was red, half stiff, of flabby fullness.

97

'Kiss me,' said the gentleman to the other girl, 'and put your tongue nicely into my mouth.' He then kissed her mouth, sucking it and glueing his mouth so hard to hers that she became breathless and red in the face. 'Oh!' he interrupted his kissing, 'play better with your tongue, you little imp'—and Grushenka could see how the blonde girl made every effort to satisfy him. But she didn't succeed entirely.

He let her go and started the same procedure with the brunette who was obediently holding his prick in her fingers. 'Let's see whether you're any better than she is.' She had a broader tongue and rubbed it slowly and more firmly against his teeth and his tongue. He grunted with pleasure. His sex feeling was swelling, but not his prick, which remained in its flabby state. It should be taken care of now, he decided.

He arose and crossed to the huge standing mirror which covered one side of the booth for the try-ons of the female customers. He threw one pillow in front of him, another one behind him. Standing sideways before the looking glass, he told the girls to kneel down on these pillows. Of course Madame had told them what to do and after they were on their knees, they pulled his trousers down to his ankles, rolled his grey silken shirt up underneath the waistcoat and got busy. The little blonde one had Master Prick before her. She took it in her right hand, put the left hand under the balls (they were quite small) and began to run her tongue over his belly, up and down the inside of the thighs, over the prick and balls. Finally she slipped the point of the penis into her mouth and started, with easy movements, to slide her lips up and down his machine, a machine by the way which still was not stiff.

Meanwhile the brunette had opened the cleft of his arse with her fingers and pressing her face firmly towards the cheeks of his behind began to tickle the rim with her able tongue. Grushenka admired her work in that respect. She even rubbed her own little pussy a bit, imagining that this good little worker was doing the same service to her lovenest. The gentleman stood straddle-legged, his hands on the heads of the girls, admiring the picture of this group in the looking glass.

He again became dissatisfied with the blonde. 'Not that way, you little bitch,' said he. 'Take just the end of the prick between your lips and tickle my little piss-hole with your tongue.' Which was duly executed.

Many minutes passed, both girls breathing heavily from their work, while he did not seem to be much affected. The brunette had already taken several intermissions in order to give her tongue a rest when suddenly he turned around, now giving her his prick to suck. The blonde stared for a moment at the arse which was presented to her. Apparently she had never rimmed a man before. But then a certain determination came to her face as if she was saying to herself, 'What's the use? We've got to dip in.'

She first rubbed the rim with her fingers to wipe off the moisture which her brunette co-worker had left there, then stretched her tongue wide out, as if to loosen it, which tickled Grushenka so that she almost laughed. The girl then buried her face in the rim and Grushenka could see by the side of her neck that she was licking. Immediately the gentleman demanded more vigour. She leaned back for a moment, glanced in the mirror and seemed to have an idea. She took hold of him again but seemingly with such passion that he was turned out of his position, almost facing away from the mirror. Of course he grumbled and said that she needed plenty of love education and that he would mention her to Madame. But she pressed her face to one of his cheeks, opened his rim with the fingers of her left hand, and began to tickle his arse hole with the little finger of her right hand, which she quickly had wet beforehand.

The result was excellent. The gentleman started groaning in praise of her ability, congratulated her on her expert tongue and worked himself up to a heat. 'Lick my arse-hole, lick my arse-hole, you little bitch! Oh, that's good, that's excellent! Why didn't you do it before, you little cocksucker …' and so on, while the blonde girl with a mixture of pride that she was cheating him and fear that he might find her out, played with her little finger on his black hole, even entering it a bit here and there.

Meanwhile the brunette had sucked and sucked and she felt that he now was coming. Not that he got stiff, but the nerves and muscles of his love-machine twisted and jerked and—there it was—his sperm flooded out. Not in a hot and thick spray, but just barely trickling out. It was not the first prick which the brunette had sucked off, in fact the Frenching business was the speciality of Madame Laura's establishment and all her girls were experts. Therefore the brunette did not mind drinking his juice, at the same time squeezing his shaft and embracing his balls tightly in order to clean him out thoroughly.

'Very good,' he murmured, pushing the girls away 'Very good.'

'Just stay where you are for a moment,' said the brunette. She got a bowl of water and a towel and did an expert job of cleaning, front and back, quite a lesson for Grushenka, who had never done this before herself. The girls now arranged his trousers properly, even brushed him up, although there was not the faintest dust on his clothes, helped him into his long coat and gave him, like good servant girls, his three-cornered hat with the feathers on it. He spoke good-heartedly with them, scolding the blonde for having teased him at first, saying that he should tell Madame. But it was all done jokingly and Grushenka could see that a very proper and well pleased gentleman left the booth with important steps as were becoming to an elderly man of standing. Before he left he gave each girl some money.

He had hardly gone, the girls were just adjusting themselves before the mirror, when Madame Laura rushed in. 'Turn over the money!' she shouted and extended her hand. 'Turn it over and back to your work or I'll speed you up.' To Grushenka's surprise, both girls gave up the money without protest. Madame Laura counted it carefully and was satisfied; for this visitor paid well. She pinched the cheeks of the girls and added smilingly, 'A funny bird, isn't he? Can't possibly get stiff and yet loves his prick. You got rid of him quickly, though. The last time the girls had an awful job until the old fool was able to come.' And she shuffled her chickens out of the room.

This whole scene had been a revelation to Grushenka . Madame Laura apparently had a side line to her dress business, a side line which attracted many customers and which she handled quite openly. The idea shot through her head that her girl friend Martha might be used for such purposes also, but then, in spite of her own predicament, she had to laugh at the thought that fat little Martha with her freshly upturned nose could be a love-maker to refined people. Of course Martha was only a sewing girl—when she stopped on the street before she brought Grushenka to Madame Laura, it must have been because she was afraid that Grushenka would be used as a 'model'—and Grushenka was fully aware again of the danger she was in. Would Madame Laura send for the police, would she be turned over to Sophia's house? But just then she heard bustling in the other compartment and went back to her look-out.

She discovered a couple shopping for a dress, a long green and fluffy evening gown which they had just bought. The woman, who held the dress in her hand and was giving orders how to change it to her liking, was about forty years of age, petite, but with an inclination to be fat. Her arms and legs, which seemed always agile, were short, round and unattractive, her swelling bosom, the upper part of which looked out of a rich afternoon gown, showed a red-brown skin. Her deep black eyes were sharp and unkind, while her lips, always pursed to an affected smile, tried to hide her true nature. She was accompanied by her husband, a husky fellow of her own age, broad-shouldered, dumb and hen-pecked. He repeated everything she said with a silly horse laugh of his own invention and seemed without a will of his own, which he probably did not need, being tied to such a mate.

A heated discussion was under way. Madame Laura excitedly praised the value of the gown, while the woman demanded a bargain in consideration of the fact that it was her first purchase in Madame's famous dress house. When a moderate sum was finally agreed upon, the woman looked

101

around towards the models and declared herself satisfied if a certain model would bring the dress to her house that evening. The girl she pointed out was a tall full-built brunette. Her unusually white skin attracted Grushenka's admiration. Madame Laura looked at this girl for a moment and hesitated, but then, with a bow, declared that the girl would be at her Ladyship's house and at her service that evening. The husband paid, with a silly laugh and a remark of his own, 'A woman must always have it her own way.' The tall girl's eyes followed the departing customers with a sheepish look.

'Are you all right, or are you still unwell?' demanded Madame Laura. The girl lifted up her dress, murmuring an indignant 'Oh!' and opening the slit of her drawers, put her fingers into her cunt from which she took a piece of cotton. It seemed clean. Madame took a small piece of white cloth, wrapped it around her finger and inserted the finger deep into the girl's vagina. Upon taking it out again, no blood could be seen.

'You fake!' shouted Madame Laura. 'Half of the time you tell me you have your menstruation and the other half of the time that you're just getting it. Backing out all the time, eh? And you have a stronger arse than any other girl here. You little liar! How long ago was it anyway, since you got your last whipping?'

'The week after Easter,' answered the girl meekly.

'Well,' retorted her mistress, 'you should get a good whipping for lying to me now but instead you'll go over to those people tonight and you'll do whatever they want—I don't know them yet—and if that Madame is satisfied with you, I'll let you go this time. But if I hear that you have not been perfect, I won't waste my time and my strength on your behind again, which is much too tough for my leather whip anyway, but I'll send you over to the police and let you have twenty-five lashes of the knout. That will cure your laziness, you tramp.'

(It must be inserted here for the understanding of the modern reader, that in Russia, servants were sent with a letter and a small fee to the nearest police station, where the requested punishment was inflicted, usually the knout over the back or over the behind. The servant then brought back to his master a receipt for the money and a short account of the punishment inflicted. This custom prevailed even in the larger cities until the end of the 19th century).

'What do you think this couple want a girl for?' asked one of the girls as they cleared the place up. The question remained unanswered.

Grushenka moved about in the semi-darkness of her cage. She didn't dare to cry out for help; she was hungry and thirsty. She remembered that the other booth had some water on a corner table. She groped around, found a similar table and a silver bowl with water in it. She drank in big gulps and returned to the couch. The minutes were creeping. She heard voices and laughter in the booths next to hers, but she did not care to peek. Then, to get her mind off her own anguish, she went back to one of the peep-holes.

The scene was worthy of her attention. The woman customer in the room presented an odd appearance. She was about thirty years of age and seemed to be more bony than muscular. She wore a riding costume with straight lines, closely fitted on the neck and wrists. She had very intelligent eyes, a hard mouth, and no colour on her cheeks which gave her an unattractive appearance. She had secured a lovely model from Madame Laura and had certainly paid enough for the right to amuse herself with her. The model was a natural blonde of medium height with full breasts and an innocent look in her face. She was quite feminine and although twenty years old, appeared almost childlike. The woman was busy taking off her bodice. She took the soft, milk-white breasts in her bony hands and admired the small nipples. Rubbing them against her cheek and sucking them playfully, she mumbled, 'You're a good girl. Aren't you? You would not allow those brutes, those men, to touch you. Would you?'

'Oh, no, never!' answered the girl. 'Never. I only wait on ladies and Madame Laura would not even allow a man to look at me.'

'Yes, such soft breasts, such small nipples, untouched,

lovely child,' continued the customer. Becoming more emotional and kneeling down before the girl, she undid her long drawers and took them off her with caressing gentleness unexpected in a woman with such large hands and feet. She then proceeded to rub her cheeks against the Mount of Venus, going up and down the sides of the girl with tender strokes of her hands.

The girl looked into the mirror, unconcerned with what the woman did to her. She teased her breasts a bit, arranged a curl which had left its place and moistened her lips with her tongue to make them look fresh and jolly. She opened her legs mechanically when the woman inserted the index finger of her right hand into her vagina and began to kiss her belly and the blonde curly hair around her pussy and gave in readily when the woman moved her over to the couch. There she stretched herself out, rolled and tucked a pillow under her head, let one leg fall down on the floor and bent herself in such a way that her open slit lay on the edge of the couch readily willing to take what was coming.

The woman now began systematically to French her, interrupting her tongue-play over and between the lips of the pussy with many poetic little outcries, as if she had found a preciously chiselled piece of jewellery. But the owner of this little masterpiece of nature did not seem to be impressed. In fact when her customer pressed her mouth vigorously to the cunt and started to suck with great force at the same time taking firm hold of the behind and pressing it forward against her strongly working tongue, the blonde rubbed her nose and smoothed her hair as if she was not even present at the treat which was being given to her love parts. Of course, now and then remembering what it was all about, she put her hand on the head of the Lesbian worker, moved her arse around in slow convulsions and ejected deep groans. But getting bored with her own behaviour, she quickly forgot to participate.

Grushenka was baffled at this coldness or rather insensibility of the blonde and sympathized with the excited woman who now pressed her knees hard together, wiggled her behind in the air, got red in the face and began to sweat in her tight fitting garments. Finally she groaned and the blonde, taking this as a sign that the climax was near, made a last effort and fucked the sucking mouth with simulated sighs of lust.

The woman customer got to her feet, her whole face wet, probably from her own saliva, while the blonde lazily brought some water and a towel and cleaned the moist and perspiring face. Her customer no longer found her the peak of loveliness. 'Well, that's that!' she said. 'You lousy slut, lying on your back for everybody who pays the price. Brats like you should be whipped daily for an hour, until they give up their brazen lives and refuse to open their legs for everybody and anybody. You're a God damned fucking cunt, that's what you are and not worth the bread you eat. Oh, well, what's the use anyway, you do it for money and here is some' and she put some money underneath a pillow, apparently as far away as possible, so as not to touch even the skin of the girl's hand. 'There! You fat pig!' and she rushed out of the room.

The words had struck home to the blonde and as she wiped her own pussy dry after the wet attack, she looked her figure over in the mirror with a scrutinizing vanity. However, Madame Laura rushed in, went straight to the pillow and got the money. 'Aha!' thought Grushenka, 'Madame is watching also, probably from the other side of the booth.'

Madame Laura was not very satisfied with the amount she found. 'You really are getting lazier every day' she turned on the girl. 'You have a new boy friend. Haven't you? And he probably fucks hell out of you. At least you could pretend better than you do. What will happen to your father and yourself if I stop paying him? You won't have a crumb of bread to eat. But maybe that will do you good, because you're getting fatter every day. Hurry up now and put some black underwear on and the white evening gown with the low neck. There are some customers in booth four. Go on now!'

There was nothing more to see in the other booth. Grushenka lay down again on her couch. The time passed. She dozed off until somebody unlocked her door and called her out. It was Martha, come to bring her back to Madame Laura's private room. Madame Laura now had a changed face. She was beaming and full of cordiality.

'My dear girl,' she smiled, 'I have been giving your case a thorough consideration and I agree that you were right to run away from Madame Sophia's service. I am going to help you and I have a great surprise in store for you. You dress now and go home for tonight with your dear friend Martha. Be here tomorrow at noon sharp and leave it to me. I'll see to it that you'll have a happy future. While I cannot allow myself to harbour a run-away, I'll have a magnificent place for you by tomorrow where you will live like a queen. Quite what you can expect, beautiful as you are …' and so on. Madame Laura even inquired whether they would have something really good to eat tonight or whether she should provide something and after the girls assured her they had all they needed, she presented Grushenka with a broad embroidered ribbon, fitting very well with the peasant dress she wore.

The girl friends curtsied and left the house. Grushenka related what she had seen, but it was no news to Martha who had heard of these things but who could not really understand their meaning because she was completely a virgin. But Grushenka lay sleepless and thinking for a long while that night. She mistrusted Madame Laura and would never go back to her. She would have to leave Martha also, without telling her where she was going. Madame Laura would probably hunt for her or send word to the police or to Sophia. Therefore Grushenka had to drop out of sight.

She did not know that Madame Laura had received an answer to her letter from an old gentleman who had written that he would be pleased to buy such a beauty from Madame Laura, but could not come before the next day at noon. He would be disappointed the next day at the noon hour and Martha would state as her explanation that Grushenka had disappeared, that she must have been picked up by the police. Madame Laura finally joined her in this belief, at least she was satisfied that Martha did not know about Grushenka's whereabouts. She was very angry about it, because she would have been able to get a good price for the sale of the girl. However, she did not want to investigate too much, because it was better not to mix into the affairs of a slave girl who had run away.

CHAPTER X.

Grushenka stretched herself in Martha's four poster bed. Martha had kissed her good-bye and left for work, admonishing her to be at Madame Laura's at noon. Grushenka slept and day dreamed. She got up lazily and put on her peasant dress, leaving her fine travelling dress in Martha's closet. She put all her money, except one ruble, on the mantel-piece, said a word of good-bye to her absent girl friend and left the house with slow steps.

She did not want to think of the future. She walked leisurely to the border of the city, went through the gate where some Cossacks loitered and found her way down to the Volga. She sat down on the bank of the river, let her eyes go over the wide plain and observed, without much attention, the peasants harvesting the fields. The waters of the wide river flowed down in easy rhythm. Far away some boys and girls were swimming.

Grushenka dreamt as only a Russian peasant can dream, a thoughtless and wordless dream, uniting herself with the soil, becoming a part of it, losing the sense of place or time. When the sun dropped lower on the horizon, she got up and slowly returned to the city. She stopped in a public house where she ate a bowl of soup and some bread and cheese. The few customers and the inn-keeper hardly noticed this peasant girl with her lovely face hidden beneath a kerchief. Back again on the street, she pulled herself up with an energetic nod of her head and walked with quick steps to Ladislaus Brenna's establishment. She had never been inside that place, but she knew all about it.

Ladislaus Brenna ran a famous bathing establishment for middle class people and Grushenka had made up her mind to become a bath attendant. She would have liked to get such a job with one of the new and elegant bath houses patronized by the fashionable world but she did not dare to do so as she might be found out. No one would look for her in Brenna's.

After she had opened the door, she stood immediately in the big bath hall for men. The hall took up the whole ground floor of the building. On a white, wooden floor stood forty to fifty wooden bath tubs in irregular arrangement. In these tubs the bather sat on a little bench, the water coming up to his neck. A few customers were bathing; others were reading, writing on little boards put over the tubs, playing board games with each other or just chatting.

Mr Brenna sat on the opposite side of the room behind an elevated bar which was covered with all kinds of refreshments and drinks. Grushenka lost no time but went right over to him while the eyes of all the bathers and attendants followed her. She stated without shyness that she wanted to become one of his bath girls. Brenna looked sharply at her and ordered her to wait. He was a whale of a fellow, about forty-five years old. His hairy chest, open to view, and his wild black beard exaggerated his tousled appearance. Grushenka sat down on a wooden bench and looked around with curiosity. She had often heard Brenna's placed discussed. It was supposed to be full of fun for its visitors, men and women alike, but most housewives disapproved violently when they heard that their husbands or grown up sons frequented it.

Grushenka's attention was first directed towards the bath attendants, about ten girls, some sitting on a bench near the big open fire-place, others moving about the big room pursuing their duties. All the girls were nude except for wooden slippers and here and there a short apron or towel around the hips. Any kind of clothes would have been annoying in this air heavy with steam and dampness. They were all husky, rather good looking girls and seemed in good spirits and satisfied. They carried buckets of hot water to the occupied bath tubs, pouring it in to keep the temperature even. They brought beer or tea or other refreshments to the men, laughed and joked with them and did not seem to mind when the men felt their breasts or their pussies. When one of the customers wanted to get out of his tub, they opened up the linen top, placed a foot stool and helped the man out. Then they followed him into one of the many cabinets which lined the walls. These cabinets had doors which closed behind the pairs and while Grushenka could not see, she could well imagine what happened inside them.

The last customer having left, the girls began to clean up while Brenna admonished them to take their time and do a thorough job. He had a gruff voice but underneath one could feel that he was a good sort. At last he turned to Grushenka and ordered her to follow him. They went upstairs, passing the women's bath hall on the second floor and passing the third floor where Brenna lived with his family. When they reached the attic, Brenna pushed open a door leading into an unoccupied room furnished with a large wooden bed, a washstand and two chairs.

'Well,' he said, 'I will look you over to see whether you are strong enough to carry the water and to give a massage. I could use a bitch like you, but you seem to be too weak. Show me what you got.'

With that he went to the little window and looked out into the twilight. His huge frame in front of the window shut out almost all the light from the room. Grushenka quickly got rid of her clothes and stood nude in the middle of the room, waiting for him to pass judgement. She was now a bit nervous. What would happen to her if he did not employ her?

Brenna gazed for quite a while out into the sunset. Finally he turned around to her, moved away from the window and put her in a position where the slowly fading light fell directly on her. He was amazed at her fine figure, her full breasts especially attracted him. Her straight legs and firm thighs did not displease him. He felt the muscles of her arms, pinched her bottom and the flesh above the knees the way one feels the leg of a horse, while she contracted her muscles as well as she could in order to appear strong. He moved her around again, uncertain whether a girl with such a small waistline would be suited to his type of work, and fixed his eyes on her Venus Hill. Grushenka was a well built girl, above medium height, but before this giant of a man she felt rather small just when she wished to be big and strapping.

Without warning he threw her on the bed so that she lay, not lengthwise, but across the bed. He opened up his linen trousers and took out a mighty and hard blown-up prick. She had hardly time to be aware of what was coming when he bent forward, rested his weight on his hands next to her shoulders, and moved his prick towards her entrance. She lowered her hands to insert his shaft and was surprised at its huge dimensions; she could hardly span it with her hand. She wanted to insert it carefully, but before she had a chance he pushed it in with a mighty stroke. Grushenka answered with a heavy groan. Not that it really hurt her, but it filled her to the utmost and stretched her cunt to the limit.

It was a few days since she had had intercourse and the scenes she had watched at Madame Laura's had also served to stimulate her desire. Therefore this unexpected attack brought her to a fever heat. She raised her legs, which still hung on the floor, high above his massive back. She thrust herself against his prick with all her power, encircling his love-instrument with the full suction of her cunt. She crushed her fingers into his muscular arms and began to fuck him with everything in her.

She closed her eyes. All kinds of lascivious pictures went through her mind; she remembered the first time she had been flogged on the bare bottom when she was fourteen years old; she thought of the peasant who had raped her and of various men who had given her satisfaction; finally the angelic features of her Mihail stood out clearly, telling her in sweet words how much he adored her.

All this time she was working with strong pushes against those of her partner while she circled her bottom around the way belly dancers do. Gradually her whole body became more and more contorted until only her shoulders touched the bed as she strove to find the best position in which to fuck and to fuck. Her body was covered with sweat, her hair became loose and partially covered her face, her mouth twisted, her heels beat his back and his buttocks. At last with an outcry the great climax came. Then she lay motionless, heavily breathing, all muscles loose. Her bottom dropped and the prick fell out of its hot nest.

Brenna lay on his hands hardly moving; he was satisfied with the vitality which this girl displayed. So satisfied, in fact, that he was not ready to let her go right now, especially since his prick was still as swollen and red as it had been.

'Eh, little hussy,' he interrupted her after-love dreams, 'Don't stop now. My little fellow down there is still stiff and angry.'

Grushenka opened her eyes to find herself staring into this gruff face surrounded with flowing black hair. An utterly strange face it was to her with black eyes, a short broad nose and full lascivious lips. Still, somehow, there was a sense of humour about it which took the sting out of its roughness. She gazed into this face and it came to her mind how much depended for her on satisfying this man. By her uncontrolled passion she had given him a wonderful time; now she would give him a still better time by her thorough knowledge of the art of fucking.

Dutifully she put her legs up on his back, this time moving them even higher, so that she almost touched his shoulders with her heels—whereby Master Prick slipped back of his own accord into his former kingdom.

She grasped his head with her hands and moved it down. His feet slid slowly backwards and he soon lay with his whole weight on her. She now lay on her back at full length and so had better means of wiggling her bottom under him. Then she arched herself under him and moving her right hand down, managed to get hold of his balls. She proceeded to caress and finger his testicles with soft strokes, at the same time tickling the inside of his ear with the little finger of her left hand.

He put his right hand under her small bottom — so large was this hand, that he was able to hold both cheeks with one clasp — and began in slow strokes to do his work. He pushed his sceptre deep into her cunt so that it touched her womb, moved slowly back to the outer entrance and repeated this play in regular rhythm. She moved her behind in circles with her eyes wide open. She was aware of every move and this enabled her to give him her fullest cooperation. When he got really hot, however, he forgot himself entirely. He got back on his feet, standing close to the bed, and raised her behind up

111

so that her head and shoulders hardly touched the linen. Holding her by her hips, he connected with her only by the contact between prick and pussy and he fucked her with all his might. She felt him come! She felt a hot flood of sperm shooting into her and strange to say, she came again.

As unexpectedly as he had attacked her, he now let her go and her behind fell to the edge of the bed. In a matter of fact way he put his still stiff prick back into his trousers. He took another look at her and liked her. Her feet touched the floor, her legs were still half open. One of her hands lay above her black-haired pussy, the coral lips of which protruded, the other hand rested on her full breast. Her mouth was a bit open, her deep black eyelashes shadowed her steel-blue eyes, her hair hung around her face. The girl was so beautiful he felt like giving her another fuck. He bent down and felt against the soft flesh of her thighs. A bit weak, yes, but his guests would like this trollop.

'Wash, and get ready for supper,' he said with resolution. 'I'll try you out. You might do.'

He opened the door and called for Gargarina. The attic was the living quarters for all the girls employed in the house and they had come up in the meantime to dress. Presently Gargarina came in and was ordered by Brenna to break in the new girl to her job. He left without further explanation.

Gargarina was an older girl, about twenty-five years of age, tall, blonde and husky. She had a shirt on and was just about to button her long lacy drawers. She looked at Grushenka with a certain curiosity. Grushenka sat on the edge of the bed, weak but not exhausted, and scratched herself thoughtfully along the soft flesh of her belly and her thighs. Gargarina opened the conversation:

'Well, he looked you over, didn't he? He certainly has the best prick in the whole neighbourhood and we ought to know. I can imagine how you feel. It's almost four years since I came here and he just killed me. After that, he told me that he could not use me. That's the way with most girls who apply for work here; he tries them all. We thought he would send you away too. You know, I just stayed on and came to work the next morning. He yelled at me to get out, but I know how

112

it is with a stray dog. He just couldn't get rid of me and that was four years ago.'

'I don't know what I would have done as I have no other place to go to either.'

'Never mind that now. It's that way with most of us girls here except those of us who were brought by their parents. One of the girls was brought by her husband. He had been drafted for the army and where could the poor creature go until his seven years are over? She don't know whether he'll ever come back. He was last heard of in Siberia. He can't write, you see, and she can't read.'

'Oh!' answered Grushenka with a flicker of pride, 'I can read and write.'

'That's fine!' retorted Gargarina kindly. 'Then you'll be able to read us some stories out of books and write our love-letters for us. You will be quite a busy person with that. But now you'd better clean out your pussy—' and she looked at the sperm which ran out of the love-nest and wet Grushenka's legs—'because you couldn't serve down in the bath hall with a swollen belly.'

She brought her a bowl of water and a towel. Grushenka sat down on the floor with the bowl, inserted a finger in her orifice, after she had wrapped the end of the towel around it, and rubbed herself, pissing at the same time. The hot gush of the piss and the rubbing of the vagina made her feel quite well and she enjoyed it. Gargarina, who was watching her, remarked. 'Tomorrow, I'll show you a better way to get your pussy clean, down in the bathing hall. But now dress quickly, dinner will be ready in a minute.'

When Grushenka came down to the dining room, she regretted that she had left her fine travelling dress at Martha's. All the other girls were dressed up fit to kill and her peasant dress looked rather out of place. There were twice as many girls as she had seen downstairs, the additional ones being those who served in the bath for women. They all sat around a long table. At one end Mr Brenna presided, at the other end sat his wife. She was a very small, thin woman of over forty, with a sharp, pointed nose, and looked like a greedy and hardened spinster. But if she was that kind, she certainly did not take it out on the girls in regard to food. Two strapping maids served a rich meal, no less good and healthy than Katerina provided for her wards. The girls hurried through their meal, anxious to leave. In fact only two or three stayed home that night, the rest having rendezvous or visiting their folks. For police identification, each girl carried a permit issued by Brenna.

Grushenka chatted with the girls remaining in the attic. She learned that room and board was all Brenna paid for their services, but that they made many, and sometimes good tips. They all were satisfied and while they were rough and used strong words they seemed to get along in good-hearted comradeship. Grushenka went to bed early and heard the girls coming home during the night.

The next morning she was up many hours before being called to breakfast. Brenna's place opened up after noon, the first guests arriving only after two or three and the whole job was done by seven in the evening. The arrival of any customer was signalled by the young fellow in the doorway, who incidentally had charge of the large stove in the basement, supplying the hot water, the heat in the wintertime and the steam for the steam room. He rapped with a stick against the door and when he rapped a few times that meant a man of money and a good tipper. All the men were more or less known to everyone.

Grushenka, taken in tow by Gargarina, lined up with the other girls near the entrance and solicited the entering man. It meant tips and the more customers a girl could get, so much the better for her. Sometimes the girls fought about the customers and that was the only thing Brenna would not stand for. He would beat them mercilessly with his fists and the girls were very much afraid of that for he would go into a rage and not take care where he hit them.

The first man who came in looked like a poet. He wore a long flowing necktie and was young and blonde. Gargarina told Grushenka not to try to attract his attention because he had a steady girl, a plump dark-haired creature with big soft breasts. This girl took him by the hand and led him into one of the cabinets where they remained for a long while.

Gargarina explained to Grushenka that he was a writer on a gazette and came every afternoon to save the soul of the dark girl. However, his sermon always ended sexually.

After him came a wealthy coachman who kept many carriages and gave good tips. All the girls besieged him, but Gargarina and Grushenka had no luck. He was followed by a master baker who was Gargarina's steady customer and the two girls went with him into a cabinet. Gargarina explained that she had to break in the 'new girl.'

The baker was a sturdy, short man, with snow white hair, bristly and unkempt. As soon as the door was closed, Gargarina started to make love to him, but he would have nothing of it. The girls undressed him leisurely taking off his coat, waistcoat, trousers and shoes. He wore no stockings but a kind of undergarment of cheap cotton which he slipped off himself. Meanwhile he told them that he was damn tired. After getting through with his baking job, beginning at nine at night and finishing at three in the morning, his old lady had awakened and had forced him to give her three rides.

His prick vouched for this statement; it hung sadly downwards. In spite of his protest Gargarina insisted on giving him a massage and he lay down reluctantly on the massage table. Gargarina took a handful of liquid soap and began to knead his flesh. She told Grushenka to do the same and while she had one side of his behind and legs in operation, Grushenka started timidly with the other half. Seeing how hard her teacher worked, she put her whole weight into her hands and soon found herself sweating. When his back was done and he was turned over, she avoided touching his testicles. This amused Gargarina, who taking the limp prick in her hand, asked Grushenka whether she would not kiss it a little and made a thousand jokes about a penis.

The baker paid no attention to this chatter. He got up from the table before they were really through with him, and walked over to a tub, which they filled with hot water. The linen was pulled over him, he leaned back and soon was soundly snoring. During the following hours, without waking him up, they kept pouring hot water into the tub, first carefully taking a bucket full of water out of it.

A few more men entered but other girls got hold of them. Then came a tall thin man whom none of the girls wanted. Grushenka held herself back instinctively. It was just her luck that he selected her. Gargarina stepped right up explaining that the new girl was under her supervision. As all three entered a cabinet together Gargarina whispered to her ward that this one was a pest.

He behaved in a very orderly way while they undressed him, told Grushenka that he was the scribe with the new judge, and that he came from Petersburg where it was the newest fad with the ladies to paint their nipples a deep red. After he was naked he embraced Grushenka, pulled her tightly to his lean body and running his long fingers up and down her spine, told her how beautiful she was and how soft her flesh felt. Meanwhile he pressed one of his thighs between hers and rubbed his prick against the soft flesh of her leg. Soon enough this love instrument became stiff and Grushenka felt that it was very thin and very long. He then proceeded to put one finger in Grushenka's cunt and began to frig her.

Gargarina had meanwhile gone behind him and embraced him from behind, rubbing her breasts on his back and her pussy on his behind. She leaned her head over one of his shoulders just as Grushenka did and both girls were almost mouth to mouth. Gargarina made faces indicating haste, but at first Grushenka did not mind his playing with her. He had apt fingers and always managed to tickle just the right spot. As she became more excited, she showed it on her face and her pussy got wet. Her arse came slowly into swing. The scribe had his other hand on her behind, but another idea struck him. He told her to take firm hold of him, and leaving one hand in her pussy, extended his other hand back until he found Gargarina's love nest and began to frig her also. Gagarina, who knew him already, fucked that finger right away as if she was terribly excited. At last he got tired of this playing around. He had another idea.

'Now, you both,' he said, 'lie down on the massage table, side by side, arse up, and I will give you a massage.' The girls did so and he began to stroke and caress their behinds, making comparisons between Gargarina's full and motherly

116

arse and Grushenka's boyish buttocks. He then went to the foot of the table and started to give both girls at the same time a rimming with his index fingers.

'Let him do it,' whispered Gargarina, putting her arm around Grushenka's shoulders and taking her breast in her hand. 'It won't hurt you'—for Gargarina already knew that they were in for a finger fuck in their arse holes. No sooner had the warning been given, than Grushenka felt him insert his long finger in her bottom hole and rub up and down, up and down.

Grushenka held still. Instead of hurting, it gave her the same feeling of longing which she had felt when Prince Leo had fucked her there. Gargarina began to wiggle around and to raise her bottom in fucking movements and Grushenka, becoming more excited, did likewise.

The thin scribe stood naked with his long prick in the air. With growing pleasure he watched the nicely moving buttocks, his disappearing and re-appearing fingers, the slightly opened arse holes, and the wide open lips of the cunts underneath. Gargarina heaved and groaned, raised herself straight up of a sudden and fell down motionless as if she had come. Grushenka repeated this fake, although she felt she would have come if she waited a bit longer. The customer let his fingers slide out and the girls sat up on the edge of the table, glad to get up from the hard boards. He stood before them and grinned, his dirty fingers outstretched before him.

'Now,' he said, 'after having massaged your cunts and your back holes, suck my fingers clean with your sweet lips and I'll give each of you one ruble.'

'Nothing doing!' countered Gargarina. 'Five rubles each and pay in advance. You forget that sometimes afterwards.'

A long squabble began between the two, he protesting that a ruble was enough money to live a week on (which was true) and Gargarina declaring that the finger sucking was not their business. They finally settled it for three rubles each, but he was allowed to play with their back holes again. While he got the money from his trousers, Gargarina got hold of some towels and whispered to her friend to be quick with them later on.

The bargain paid for, they sat down on the edge of the

table, raised their knees high up, put their feet on the table and opened up. From underneath, he again stuck both his index fingers into their arse holes and began the finger fucking anew, much to the satisfaction of his long, thin prick, which had shown an inclination to droop during the money quarrel, but which now raised its head proudly. Grushenka again felt her pussy getting wet and glancing at the play of flesh of Gargarina's strong thighs, she saw that her teacher apparently was also becoming heated up.

Meanwhile the scribe's mouth watered and he babbled on to the effect that their pretty lips would soon suck the fingers which were now playing in the dirty back alley. Finally he got through with their bottoms, took his fingers out and pointed them at the girl's mouths. Quick as lightning Gargarina grabbed his hand and cleaned his fingers off with her towel, despite his protest, and of course Grushenka quickly followed her example. Although he swore wickedly they then took his fingers in their mouths and sucked them.

Grushenka at first had a sickening feeling and would never have done it had not Gargarina set the example. But strangely enough, when the finger was moving back and forth in her mouth it aroused the same feeling of longing and desire as it had done before in her behind.

The scribe's face turned crimson and Grushenka's eyes, sliding down to his prick, saw how Gargarina had skilfully grasped his long tail between her feet. She was rubbing it gently in this manner. After a little while of this play, he came suddenly, shooting out a flood of white sperm in great gushes. He immediately took his fingers out of their mouths, took his prick in both hands and finished himself off, emptying his balls to the last drop.

No sooner was this done than he began to talk about the money, which he demanded back, threatening to report them to Mr Brenna for stealing. But the money had disappeared and Gargarina laughed at him. She had hidden it in her hair and took it out of there, to Grushenka's amazement, when she later gave her her share. After that, they laid him on the table and gave him a rough massage. He struggled and screamed under their hands—it was a little revenge on their part. When they had finally seated him in his tub, he read a big manuscript of legal matters and behaved very importantly. Then both girls went back to sit on the bench near the stove to await a new customer.

Gargarina advised her new girl friend that the scribe was as bad a customer as they were likely to get. He was hard to handle but had they not got ten times more money out of him than any other man would pay and wasn't that the main thing? Seeing that Grushenka rubbed her pussy with her palm, she laughed and remarked that they probably would still get plenty of good pokes before the day was over, because that was what most of the men did who came there.

She was right. the next man they had was a young stone mason and Grushenka soon felt the hard boards of the massage table under her back and shoulders while a young prick pumped away in her hole. Gargarina looked playfully on, teasing her breasts and behind with her expert fingers. After the mason they had an elderly inn keeper who wanted a ride, half of which was provided by Gargarina, while he sucked Grushenka's nipples, the other half by Grushenka's cunt, which did the job excellently, remembering its exercises over the fat Sokolow's love shaft. He proved a good tipper but had a distasteful habit; he smacked their behinds lustily with his fat hands and when Grushenka tried to avoid this, he gave her what he termed, 'A little love spanking.'

They had other men—all of them curious about Grushenka because she was a 'new girl.' But after a few weeks Grushenka became just one more of Mr Brenna's attendants, and while she was pretty and a good love partner, she had days when she attended the men without any lovemakings. Other days, of course, she had to be of service several times. She did not mind it.

One fuck, however, she received daily and there was something curious about that. Each day since she had started to work for Mr Brenna, as soon as the customers had gone, he walked up to her room and fucked her exactly as he had done the first time. In fact he became enamoured of her. He watched her constantly when she worked in the bath hall, until she sometimes felt uneasy of his lurid eyes always focused on her spot. Brenna had never before had a favourite among his girls, and it became the gossip of the whole establishment that he had fallen for her. He did not interfere with her in any way; seldom spoke with her; let her take care of the customers; let her go out in the evenings; but always before dinner he followed her upstairs and poked her with his tremendous machine. She gave him her best. She took care of the customers in a more or less routine way, but she clung to his prick with all the vitality and sacrifice of her young cunt.

During this time she had many amusing evenings. The girls took her out to some parties, usually with young boy friends, sailors, students and the like. They would sit around in the dark public parks or on house stoops and occasionally in the rooms of the boys where they drank heavily of vodka, delivered enthusiastic orations about the rosy future, or were just busy love making. A young student, the son of poor parents, fell in love with Grushenka and she felt very flattered because he was so educated. He told her all about his studies and how they would marry when he made money and they could settle down. It was not a romance on her part, because she still dreamt only of her Mihail. Yet it was pleasant to be adored by such a clean boy. That was about all the feeling she got out of it, because he had big, red hands, was awkward and shy and did not even dare to kiss her. When she embraced him once, he got so terrified that he avoided her for days and then lectured her to the effect that only man and wife, being duly married, could kiss each other. If he had only known what her occupation was and what her life had been so far!

Grushenka felt curiously happy. She had forgotten her fear of being detected by Madame Sophia and had saved up a little money, tied in a kerchief. She bought fine material and made herself dresses and coats and skirts, she was on good footing with the other girls—nothing was lacking. But one evening the following occurred.

As usual she lay across her bed and Mr Brenna had his good love-instrument in the right place and both were working away at their best when the door opened and Madame Brenna entered. She watched the scene for a moment without their having heard or seen her. Then she rushed forward, yelling and screaming and began to beat her unfaithful husband's huge back with her bare fists. Of course he let Grushenka go and turned around, his big yard sticking out accusingly. But the thin little Madame Brenna had not done with him yet. Yellow with rage, she showered him with blows, biting his hands, which he held out against her to shield himself, scratching his face and tearing his clothes. He could have knocked her down with a single stroke of his powerful arms, but he was so scared and in awe before his rightful wife that he took it all without protest. Finally she pushed him out of the door, kicking him down the stairs, all the while letting him know that she would not stand for his giving another girl what was rightfully coming to her.

After she had gone Grushenka remained in a daze on her bed. What would be her fate now? Would that woman kill her, would she beat her mercilessly, would she have to leave the house, would she be adrift again? She wondered and did not dare to dress to go down to dinner. Finally she heard steps at her door and when she sat up in bed, Madame Brenna came in. She was very calm now and almost friendly.

'It was not your fault,' began Madame Brenna. 'What could you do? You had to fuck him. I understand that. When his father gave me a job here some twenty years ago and the son started to fuck me, I couldn't object either. Then he married me. That big brute! But never let it happen again. Will you promise me that? Swear it to me!'—and Grushenka swore it.

'All right then, and if he tries again, you run away and come right down stairs. I'll fix him up. Understand? You'll not work for him again downstairs. You start tomorrow in the woman's department—and keep away from him or next time I'll break every bone in your body!'—and making a gesture showing that she would tear her to pieces, Madame Brenna left the room with resolute steps. She had more energy, thin and small as she was, then Grushenka had expected.

CHAPTER XI.

Grushenka was somewhat downcast with this verdict. It would have been better if she had received a good licking and had stayed in the men's department. First of all she liked men and not women, and secondly Madame Brenna was quite severe with her girls. She had mostly serf girls working for her and their backs, bottoms and thighs often showed signs of harsh treatment. What should Grushenka do—quit? Then what? She gave in and reported at the women's department the next noon. The equipment of this bathing hall was almost the same as that downstairs, except that on the floor and in the cabinets, were some runners and rugs. Madame Brenna sat behind an elevated desk where she sold tea and cakes instead of beer and vodka. But she did not stay behind her bar as her husband always did. No, she ran about all the time, seeing to it that cabinets were cleaned up after a customer left, chatting and gossiping with the women in the tubs and ceaselessly admonishing the girls to keep busy. With her commanding words, usually went a pinch on the arm or on the bottom.

The girls lined up at the door when a customer came in. Each tried to get as many as possible, because of the tips. The customers were of the same kind as the men, middle class women of all ages. Many came only for a hot bath because there were no bathing facilities in the houses of the middle class of that time. Some of them wanted a massage and a rest and many of them, not having any serfs at home, wanted something more. But all of them used the attendant bath girls as their private property, as serfs, rented for a time and on whom they could let their fancy go as it would.

Grushenka realized this with her first customer. This patroness was a young girl of about Grushenka's age, whose father had recently made some money with a pottery business. While this father refused to allow his family an elegant household with servants and the luxury of the upper class, there was enough cash available for his daughter to behave the thorough snob outside her four walls. She was decked out in a cloak with golden threads woven into it, her shoes had big silver buckles and she looked like a real lady.

When she came in she eyed the ten girls who stood there naked and smiling. She took her lorgnette and slowly and carefully looked them over. Grushenka felt a chill when the eyes of this young girl wandered from her bust down to her belly and then down to her spot and over her legs. She was not so happy when she was selected. She did not know why, because this young girl had a harmless and friendly face, though around her mouth were lines of haughtiness and disgust.

She led her customer to a cabinet, closed the door and began devotedly to undress her. The girl stood perfectly still and did not make a move, not even opening a ribbon or slipping out of a single garment. Grushenka found it best to admire loudly all of her wearing apparel although she met only with the answer that it was very costly and that Grushenka should lay each piece out or hang it up with great care. The girl demanded her hair undone and braided, so that it should not get wet. Meanwhile, she sat before the mirror studying her face and her decidedly good figure.

After her hair was done, Grushenka asked whether she desired a massage and which way she wanted it. Instead of an answer, the girl turned around and began to study Grushenka's form and features. She became jealous of Grushenka's full and even bust, her subtle waist, her straight belly and good legs. Of a sudden she put a finger into Grushenka's pussy, shoved it all the way in, and drawing her nearer asked:

'All men are crazy about your spot—aren't they?'

'Oh no!' answered Grushenka instinctively. 'Oh, no! Men usually don't like me.'

'Not much, you liar,' sneered the fair patroness and letting her finger slip out of the hole, she gave her a resounding slap

123

on the thigh.

Grushenka drew back, holding her smarting spot with her hands and groaning, 'Oh, Oh—please don't do that!'

'Why not? Why shouldn't I give you a sound spanking if I like to?' retorted the girl with a sneer. 'Didn't I hire you for my pleasure? Since when can I not do with Madame Brenna's girls what I like? Shall I call her in and ask her?'

'Please don't call Madame Brenna,' answered Grushenka timidly. 'I'll do everything you want me to—but please don't hurt me. You don't need to pay me if you don't want to,' she added.

'We'll see about that, you little serf girl,' replied the customer. 'Now come here and turn around and bend over—yes, so—that's all right. And don't dare to move away or I'll teach you!'

With that remark, she began to pinch Grushenka's bottom. First she took the flesh of the right cheek between the thumb and index finger, squeezing the soft flesh firmly and turned her hand around. Grushenka put her own hand to her mouth so as not to cry out aloud, for it hurt her terribly. She leaned forward, trembling in her legs. The girl watched with pleasure. The pinched spot first turned snow white and then deep red.

'Now you look all uneven,' she remarked. 'We can't stand for that—' and she pinched the left cheek of the arse in the same way. Not content with that, she attacked different points above and beneath the bruised area and admired her handiwork with laughter.

Grushenka suffered under each pinch as if fire burnt her backside. Between pinches, the girl reached through Grushenka's open legs and pulled the hair of her Venus Hill, not very hard, but hard enough to make her groan aloud. Meanwhile Grushenka had the feeling that she had to piss. But she was afraid to piss over the customer's hand—Madame Brenna's whip would have been the consequence. Then the girl got bored with her doings.

'Sorry,' she said, 'That we haven't a whip or a switch here. Otherwise I would erase the nice design which I made on your bottom.' Grushenka straightened out and turned around. The girls eyes were fastened to her full breasts. 'How I'd love to whip your breasts,' she went on, 'with a small leather strap, the one I have at home for my lap dog. It would be a pleasure to see your breasts, of which you're so proud, prettily striped with the lash. You see I don't like to hit you with my hands because that hurts me and wouldn't go through your thick skin anyway, you slut.'

Nevertheless, she made Grushenka hold her breasts with both hands while she struck her a couple of times with bare hands. Grushenka was able to catch these slaps with her hands, but it stung her anyway not a little. This over, the girl demanded her satchel, out of which she took a large artificial penis. She laid herself on the massage table, opened up her legs, had Grushenka stand close to her, and gave her the phallus. Grushenka opened up the lips of the cunt with her left hand and with her right, she carefully sunk the artificial prick into the vulva.

The girl became very passionate. She put her right hand between Grushenka's thighs, near the cleft, and clamped her hand into the flesh, sinking the nails into Grushenka's soft skin. At the same time, she held her left hand tight on her own well-formed bosom and worked her bottom against the prick in a quick rhythm. Grushenka duplicated this rhythm by easing the prick into the hole up and down. The girl breathed heavily, whispered the name of her imaginary lover and moved her bottom up higher and higher until when she reached her climax she rested only on her shoulders and on the soles of her feet. She fell back on the table and lay motionless while Grushenka removed the intruding shaft and cleaned the pussy with a wet towel. She was glad it was over, but that proved a mistake. As soon as the girl came to, she had another scheme.

'Give me the prick!' she commanded. 'And you go down and give my sweet pussy a good licking and don't stop before I tell you. Understand? No, that's not the right spot. Stick out your tongue, you stupid fool! Deeper! Yes, that's it.'

Grushenka had her head buried between the thighs of this newly rich girl who revenged her own poor childhood with its many whippings and humiliations by taking it out on

125

another girl. Grushenka had not practised using the tip of her tongue for some time, and although she knew how she had formerly done it, she worked too quickly and pressed her mouth too hard into the open vulva, so that she soon was breathless and her tongue became sore.

The girl had crossed her legs behind Grushenka's neck and pressed her tightly against her pussy. She was not yet excited because she had just come under the pressure of Master Prick. This dildo she held playfully in her hands, placing it between her breasts, tickling her nipples, finally kissing it all along the shaft and then inserting it into her mouth and sucking it with delight. She did not concentrate on the feelings of her pussy beyond the agreeable tickling which Grushenka's tongue play produced. Grushenka stopped for a moment, getting her breath and resting her tongue, and looking up saw the penis disappearing and re-appearing from the mouth. The fair sucker was not willing to let her have a rest and hit her on the back with the soles of her feet.

Grushenka resumed her occupation. This time she held the pussy open with her left hand and, coming from underneath, inserted the index finger of her right hand in the vulva and massaged the sheath all the way along until the womb seconded the efforts of her tongue to make the little love place spend. This method apparently met with the approval of the buttocks, because they started to move up and down, first slowly, then increasing their tempo to such a degree that Grushenka had a hard time keeping the tip of her tonge exactly at the right spot.

However, it was the desire of her patroness to prolong the play. She twisted away, even took the priceless shaft out of her mouth and ordered Grushenka to stop. But Grushenka hung on. She kept her mouth close to the cunt and sucked with all her might. Finally the girl gave up fighting and came. She lay panting while Grushenka took a soft towel and rubbed her legs, belly, breast and arms removing the sweat and giving her at the same time a strengthening massage. Her customer had her eyes closed and seemed to sleep. Grushenka was about to leave, when the girl got up lazily, gave her a malicious look and started for the door. Grushenka thought she was going to the tub. Instead, the girl opened the door and motioned Madame Brenna, who, always on the watch, came swiftly inside.

'I always pay well and you know I never complain,' said the girl, 'but look at this serf here. She is so lazy that when I tell her to kiss me a little, she just gives me words. I don't care what you do about it, but you know there are the aristocratic bath halls where I should have gone in the first place …'

'Is that so?' asked Madame Brenna with a grin and a severe look in the direction of Grushenka. 'I'll wake the bitch up, if you permit. Come here Grushenka and lie over this chair. Yes, the bottom up.'

Grushenka did as told. Her head hung down; her hands held the legs of the chair with an anxious grip; her poor behind was turned up. Madame Brenna took a towel, held it in water until it was soaking wet and put her left hand firmly on Grushenka's back. She saw the marks of the pinching and guessed the rest of the story, making up her mind to fake the beating. But Grushenka, trembling and weeping and protesting her innocence, now lost control of herself entirely. She not only felt like pissing, nay, she pissed! In a big stream the yellow liquid ran out of her pussy and over her thighs onto the carpet.

The girl laughed aloud. After the sadness and bad mood which had followed her two orgasms, she now felt delightfully happy. Madame Brenna, however, became really angry. The wet towel proved to be a more painful instrument than a switch or a leather strap. While the latter gave the kind of stinging cut suggested by its switching sound through the air, the wet towel gave only a thud when it hit, but it crushed the flesh, inflicting the pain of a contusion. Madame Brenna understood how to handle a wet towel on a naughty girl's bottom. She had perfected herself through over a score of years and Grushenka's behind was just another arse to her.

'Such a lousy girl, to piss on that good rug,' she thought, and Grushenka's behind was soon purple red from the knees to the small of the back. She howled and squealed like a pig being killed. She tossed about in her awkward position, her tear-dimmed eyes fixed on her own knees which she saw underneath the chair seat. On her body, arched so that the behind was its highest point, the blows rained with awful strength—swap—swap—swap!

Madame Brenna did not count the strokes. Grushenka had roused her anger and she'd know when it was time to stop. The girl customer looked on, highly amused. While she still laughed about the peeing business, a glea of perverted passion glowed in her eyes and a feeling of satisfaction crept through her loins. 'Oh, if father would only buy some serf girls,' she thought, 'I'd beat them myself—but with a good leather whip, not with a wet towel.' She herself had felt the switch and the strap not so many years ago when her father was still poor and she was the hired maid of a rich market woman. And how often the leather whip had cut her young breasts—and in recollection, she caressed her full bust with both hands, reassuring herself that those times were over forever.

Meanwhile Madame Brenna had finished her job and motioned her customer out of the cabinet and into a tub. Grushenka let herself fall from the chair and lying on her stomach felt her sore backside with careful fingers. This indulgence, however, was short lived. Madame Brenna soon was back again and made her clean up the room. Taking her roughly by the arm, she dried her face with a handkerchief and tied up her ruffled hair.

'Not another sob!' she said, 'or I'll start again. Pull youself together and go after your work. You see,' she added maliciously, 'that's what comes of getting the biggest man of the neighborhood to squeeze it into you; you can't even hold your water.'

Grushenka subdued her sobs. Under Madame Brenna's orders, she carried hot water for re-filling the tubs, she cleaned out a tub and so on. While Grushenka's arse hung heavy with pain, she was given no time to sulk and mope.

Furthermore, she soon had to take care of a customer of another kind. A middle-aged woman of a motherly type selected her; a woman with kind eyes and ruddy complexion, more stout than fat, more big than tall. While she undressed her, Grushenka admired her firm flesh, her large hard bust, her muscular legs. The woman stroked Grushenka's head, called her all kinds of sweet names, complimented her on her lovely features and body and did not seem the least bit jealous of her beauty. After she was naked, she asked Grushenka to wash her pussy. When this was duly done she said, 'Now, my sweet darling, please be a dear and give me a long good sucking. You see my old man hasn't touched me in over five years. I don't know whether he could find his way anymore, if he wanted to, and I can't help craving some excitement. You see every so often it tickles me down there and so I come here once a week and have my little hothouse regaled with the play of an apt tongue like yours, and remember, I enjoy it most when a girl is willing and beautiful as you are.' With this, she moved Grushenka's head, carefully and with caresses, between her big thighs.

Grushenka started the job. She had plenty of operating field before her. The woman spread her big legs wide open; the small part of the belly, both sides of the cleft, the over-developed Venus Hill received soft kisses and slow ticklings with the tongue while Grushenka's well-formed hands gently took hold of the big buttocks. Grushenka took the large long lips of the grotto in her mouth alternately and sucked them, even biting them tenderly. Then she turned her efforts towards the main object, namely the large but juicy vagina.

The woman lay still except that her fingers tried to tickle Grushenka's ears, but Grushenka shook them off. When, however, the tongue nipped the clitoris, licked around it and pressed and massaged it with stronger strokes, the woman changed her behaviour. She began to heave and to toss with passion and her sweet words turned into sharp curses. Grushenka could not make out what she whispered so hoarsely, but words like 'take your damed prick away' or 'you lousy old cock-sucker' turned up repeatedly in this randy monologue. When she finally came, the woman closed her strong legs behind Grushenka's head, drawing her so tightly towards her cunt as to almost suffocate her. Releasing her, she sat up on the table, scratched her fat belly thoughtfully and muttered more to herself than to Grushenka: 'It's a shame for an old woman and a mother of a grown up daughter—but what can you do?' Soon she sat in her tub, a respectable elderly woman with kind looks and refined behaviour. Grushenka received a good tip from her.

Grushenka was greeted with many sarcastic remarks from the other customers and girls wherever she passed. Her first patroness had told the story of her pissing on the floor and all the women considered it a huge joke. This same patroness annoyed and vexed her again when she was through with her bath. After she had been dried, an operation during which she found many faults with Grushenka and during which she pinched her with her sharp fingernails under the arms and in the sensitive flesh of the breasts (of which she was jealous) she had another one of her striking ideas.

'You little pisser! You know what you are good for? As a piss-pot! Come, sit down on the floor and I will piss in your mouth.'

Grushenka did not obey. She brought a piss-pot from the corner and put it down. The girl clutched Grushenka's hair around the pussy and raising her right hand threatened to hit her. But Grushenka remained firm.

'I shall yell for Madame Brenna,' she said and stood her ground. The girl wavered.

'What else do you do,' she retorted, 'but eat cunts all day long? Why should you, you of all people, refuse to drink a little piss?' Grushenka struggled free and went to the other side of the massage table.

'I believe, Madame,' she said, 'that another girl wil serve you better than I can. May I call another one?' The girl shrugged her shoulders.

'No! No!' she muttered and had herself dressed without another word. Ready to go, she took a ruble's worth of coins out of her purse. Grushenka reached for it, but the girl had decided to give it to her in another manner.

'Wait,' she said. 'Lie down on the table and open up. I'll put it in your hole as a cork to stop the leak.'

Grushenka did as she was told, hoping thus to get rid of her tormentor more quickly. She held her pussy as wide open as possible so as not to get hurt when the silver was slipped in. The girl, who already had her gloves on, opened the slit with two fingers and for a moment examined this finely made love nest. The lips were rosy and oval, the opening lay deeper than her own and in close neighbourhood to the clearly visible back hole. The sheath seemed narrow and the tickler, being near the entrance, raised its head freshly. 'What a treasure of a cunt,' she thought, 'Really, I never would lick a pussy, but this one—'

Grushenka moved nervously; her tender parts lay open to the aggression of this patroness whom one could not trust. The girl slipped the coins in, first the small silver coins which had a higher value, then the big copper coins worth one or two copecks. She had quite some fun when these pieces did not go in so easily, while Grushenka trembled anxiously, not hurt, but afraid of what still might come. Finished, the girl slapped her with her gloved hand over the open hole. Grushenka jerked her legs together and jumped from the table, while the girl laughingly remarked from the door: 'Keep it there and you won't get broke.'

During the many weeks Grushenka worked in the women's department, she found out that women are crueller and meaner than men. The women had no humour or fun on their minds; they wanted to be satisfied, utterly selfishly. They complained without cause and having power over their attendants, they tormented and vexed them without reason and very often unexpectedly. They might be very nice and considerate and all of a sudden pinch her or call for Madame Brenna to punish her. They tipped not half as well as the men did and called attention to it heavily when they parted with a few copecks. None of them ever kissed her pussy or made love to her, while many requested that she bring their elderly ticklers to the climax. Grushenka did not mind that. She soon learned to work her tongue over their bodies or their pussies in a routine way, hardly considering what she was doing and faking passion and eagerness when she felt that her patronesses were about to spend. But what got her nervous was that she never knew when Madame Brenna would find fault with her and punish her.

These punishments were of all kinds. Madame Brenna would whip her soles with a leather strap when she had not moved with enough alacrity; she would hit her breasts with a switch when a customer complained that she had admired herself in the mirror; she would tie stinging nettles on the inside of Grushenka's thighs or on her bare behind when she was tired or drowsy.

While none of the women customers made love to her, they always liked to rub their thick fingers in her sheath, not in a friendly and teasing way, but roughly, as if they wanted to enlarge her wonderfully small passage. Unconsciously, perhaps, they were envious because Grushenka had the narrowest hole of them all.

Grushenka thought that Madame Brenna kept after her more than after the other girls because she was still angry about her husband. That was wrong. But her conscience was soon especially uneasy and for a good reason. One evening when she had been in the woman's department only a few days and, through with work, had just reached her room, Mr Brenna came in. As was his habit, without saying a word, he threw her over the bed and gave her one of his tremendous pokes. She did not dare to fight him or to yell for help. She just gave in, gasping. She did not enjoy his big shaft for she kept watching the door, dreadfully afraid that they might be detected.

The next day he came again and from then on every day. As things seemed to go smoothly Grushenka finally forgot her fear and concentrated again on his love power which filled her with hot chills and stimulated her to the climax of sacrificing passion. This went on for weeks and then, of course, one fine day Madame Brenna stood in the room again and the same scene as before repeated itself. Only this time, after having beaten up her husband, Madame Brenna gave Grushenka a murderous look, drove her husband out of the room, went herself, slammed the door behind her and locked and bolted the door from the outside.

For a moment Grushenka was horrified. She sat on the edge of the bed, paralysed, unable to move or to think. Then an idea flashed through her brain, an idea that drove her to feverish activity. Flight! Away! As quickly as possible, as quick as lightning. She dressed, wrapped her clothes into a bundle and stuck the kerchief with the money into her bodice.

Flight! How to leave the room? The oak door did not budge. The lock was of forged iron. But there was the window! Through the window, over the window sill, along the house ledge into the open window of the next room. A dash through that room, flight down the stairs, out of the house, along the street, around the first corner, the second, the next.

Exhausted and with a beating heart, Grushenka leaned against a house wall. Nobody had followed her. Still breathless, she forced herself to move on. The twilight turned to darkness. She reached Martha's house and the girl friends kissed each other tenderly and with tears. For a long time, neither spoke a word.

CHAPTER XII.

The stay with Martha was brief. The little money Grushenka had went quickly. Grushenka did not want to be a burden to her friend. She had to think of the future. She had found out from Martha that Mme. Laura once had a scheme to dispose of her and she resolved to try Mme. Laura again. Without telling Martha about it, she got ready one day at noontime and was soon sitting in Mme. Laura's private office.

Mme. Laura took little time to scold her for running away, but she asked Grushenka if she would this time accept what was provided for her. Grushenka consented meekly. Thinking it over, Mme. Laura dispatched a letter, this time to another gentleman. Grushenka sat in a corner of the office and waited. About an hour later Mme. Laura returned with a man about thirty years old. Dressed like a dandy, with a face like an Italian, his moustache was twirled up audaciously. He seemed coarse and vain and of a false hilarity. His hands were covered with dazzling diamonds.

'Here is a beautiful model of mine,' Mme. Laura said, pointing at Grushenka. 'One of my serf-girls. I want to get rid of her because I promised a poor dear relative of mine her place. Now if she were just one of the usual run I would not have sent for you, but she is one of the finest and most beautiful creatures I have ever seen. As you are a connoisseur of women and always on the lookout for special beauties, I thought I had better send for you.' She looked searchingly at the man. He twirled his moustache with affected fingers. He hardly looked in Grushenka's direction.

'One more or one less, it doesn't matter with us.' He seemed bored.

'Come here, my dove,' Mme. Laura made Grushenka get up and step forward. 'Show yourself to the gentleman.'

Grushenka stood before him, Mme. Laura tenderly stroking her hair and turning her slowly around. His face was expressionless. When Grushenka stood with her back towards him, she felt Mme. Laura slowly raising her dress, her petticoats, then flattening out her drawers so as to expose her behind. The gentleman seemed pleased. 'Oh,' he said, 'you know my taste, don't you. Always give your customers what they ask for, eh? You know damn well that I like well formed, small behinds, not those big fat arses with their fat bolsters which are always in the way.' And he laughed in falsetto.

When he heard that the price was only a hundred rubles, he took a handful of loose gold out of his pocket, threw ten pieces on the table with a move of his hand as if to say, 'a hundred rubles—bah, what's that'—and Grushenka was sold. Needless to say, Mme. Laura made the money disappear, not with undue haste, oh no, but quick enough to be sure that she had got every bit of it.

At the door waited a princely carriage. The man got in and had Grushenka sit down with him on the front seat. Grushenka wondered at a master driving through Moscow with a serf sitting next to him on the driver's seat of the carriage.

The answer to this came soon enough. Grushenka learned all about it while she had her first meal. Serge, that was his name, had been a serf himself. Now he was major domo to the old Prince Asantschejew—not only major domo but his jailor and tormentor. The old Prince was entirely at his mercy. He was kept a prisoner in his own bed, was not allowed to see any of his relatives or friends, was in fact held incommunicado. Serge had made himself master by trickery and sheer physical strength and had set himself up as tyrant over the wasted estate of the old Prince. He had forced his master to liberate him and in his last will to bequeath him a sizeable farm and some money. He had not dared to stipulate too large an amount for fear that after the death of the Prince the heirs and relatives would throw over the document and take their revenge on him. Therefore he kept the old man alive in order to steal as much cash as possible from the estate before his death.

Serge was an excellent administrator. By tolls and taxes he

knew how to squeeze their last penny out of the farmer-serfs of the estate. But the household was run in a very disorderly manner, every servant doing just about what he wanted to do. The house, a tremendous castle, was unclean, the servants were dressed in rags, the horses were not cared for or properly fed, the whole little community of over fifty people lingered around without plan or discipline. Serge did not give a damn. He went about cursing and swearing, a short leather whip hanging from his belt always ready to strike—but only because he was concerned with his own comfort.

'What does he do with so many good looking girls?' asked Grushenka. 'Well,' they answered, and grinned, 'You'll find that out in time.'

After dinner and a bath, Grushenka was first of all able to save her own clothes. They were not burned as usual and she was happy, for she had bought them with her own money. The elderly housekeeper then said that she had to give her the usual thrashing, but Grushenka wiggled herself out of that too by flattering the woman, kissing the switch and just making her forget to use it on her. But now she was a serf-girl again. The price for her liberty was in the purse of Mme. Laura.

Serge forgot about Grushenka after her arrival and she behaved like all the other serfs in the house. When they heard him approaching a room—and he was usually shouting and yelling—they quickly fled before he could see them. She never saw the old Prince Asantschejew. Only two elderly women were allowed to enter his room, women trusted by Serge because they too had been taken care of in the Prince's will.

One day Serge missed one of his rings. He was in a rage. The ring seemed to have been stolen by one of the women (he kept no male serfs in the house and never had visitors). He ordered all the women into the biggest room of the basement and shouted that if the ring were not returned he'd kill every one of them to be sure that he didn't miss the thief. One of the girls suggested that she had seen the ring on a sideboard upstairs, and a few girls, including Grushenka, went to that room with him. There the ring was found.

But meanwhile Serge had laid his eyes on Grushenka.

Grushenka was dressed in a blouse and petticoat without skirt or drawers. Her legs were bare and she wore wooden slippers. It was her working costume. As he looked at her, Serge's eyes sparkled.

'You are Mme. Laura's girl, aren't you?' he said, and he put one hand under her petticoat on her bare bottom, while his other hand stroked her thighs and the flesh of her belly but without touching her pussy. 'Well, well, I forgot all about you. But no time is better than the present. Kneel straddle-legged on that easy chair and bend over, my chicken.'

Grushenka did as she was told, put her knees on the arms of the wide easy chair and bent over a bit. She expected to get poked. The other girls watched him with malicious smiles. But Serge was not quite satisfied. He grabbed her by the neck and bent her forward until her head touched the seat of the chair, doubling her up to the utmost. One of the girls threw Grushenka's petticoats up and over her back, and Grushenka could see through her opened legs how Serge took his sizeable shaft out of his dirty linen trousers. She went with her right hand to her cunt, parted the lips with a quick move of the fingers and held it open awaiting the attack.

'A nice, clean arse,' remarked Serge. 'Sorry I forgot so long about it.'

He moved forward, got hold of her loins, and glancing down, approached her with the tip of his shaft. Grushenka reached for his love-instrument, but he shouted for her to take her hand away. He then began to press his prick against her back-hole.

He was an arse-fucker by conviction and inclination. First of all he did not want his girls to become pregnant. Furthermore he found the back-hole smaller and tighter. Finally he did not want to give his girls a thrill; he liked to do his fucking himself and to spin out his amusement as long as possible without the help of his partner.

Thus the head of Serge's shaft now engaged in a struggle to enter Grushenka's small back-hole. He pressed, screwed and pushed. It pained her. Not that she was still a virgin back there. Prince Leo had initiated her arse hole, more than one finger had rubbed and entered it. Serge however did not use any ointment nor did he direct or help with his hand, and she groaned and sighed under his lengthy attack. He was expert in entering a back-hole. He knew that the muscle holding it tight was on top, and he massaged this muscle with his pressure. It gave way and his shaft entered in full.

After he had it all in he paused a moment, got himself into a comfortable position and began a slow fucking. Grushenka, glancing through her legs at his big brown hairy balls and the end of the appearing and disappearing shaft, wanted to help along and wiggled her bottom. But he slapped her on the thigh and commanded her to hold still. She felt his machine grow bigger and bigger, she felt like taking a good shit, she felt that empty longing in her cunt, while the minutes crept by. The other girls stood around and whispered.

Finally he came, not speeding up his movements at all and not withdrawing his prick afterwards. He just stood and waited until it became small and soft and slipped out by itself. Then he left the room without a word. He had hardly left when the girls burst into a babble of comment and hilarity. The remarks flew through the room:

'Well, another virginity and no blood shed ...'

'I want to be Godmother in nine months.'

'I always play with my finger, when he sticks it into my arse.'

'He would not take me, my veranda protrudes too much'—displaying a very muscular and fat behind with such a tight cleft that the back-hole could not be seen.

'He usually lines three or four girls up in a row, has them bend down as you did just now, and goes from one hole to the other.'

'Be careful not to wiggle your behind; when he comes too quickly, he'll beat you to a bloody mess.'

'And don't put salve into your cleft. He wants to force the entrance and hates an easy hole.'

'You'll be on his list from now on. I could see he liked your buttocks.'

'Oh, if I only had a good prick—right now—for my little pussy!'

'Have yourself sent to the stable for a thrashing. The boys

138

won't hurt you, but they'll fuck you all right.'

'I can loan you my finger, if that will help you out.'

'Why not take a candle?'

It was done as said. The girls were excited after seeing Grushenka get fucked. Serge never allowed them to go out of the house and they could hardly ever manage to get a prick in the right spot. The girl who was the leader of the chorus lay on the couch. Another girl took a big candle from one of the side-brackets and filled the longing love-nest with intensive pushes. They had done this often before. They had found out who had the longest vagina, making a mark on the candle for each cunt, and they were clever in satisfying each other in this way.

Grushenka, who watched with interest as each girl took her turn to lie down on the couch, felt rather randy. In the group was a very young girl, not much more than fifteen or sixteen years old, very blonde and delicate. She would not let herself be pushed but she caressed the faces and breasts of those girls wiggling under the candle. Grushenka put her arm around her and whispered in her ear. 'Will you do to me what I do to you—everything?'

The girl shyly nodded her consent. Grushenka laid her on the carpet, rolled her petticoats up and began to smother her soft belly with kisses. The girl was ticklish and giggled. Grushenka opened her young legs and buried her head between the girl's thighs. The pretty little pussy was still almost without hair. The girl was fighting against the intruder, not earnestly, yet struggling a bit, and this made Grushenka still more anxious to suck this cunt with all the ability she had acquired during her stay in Mme. Brenna's bath establishment.

The girl sighed and heaved and tossed about, entwining herself with Grushenka's sucking mouth when the climax came. The girl was, in fact, a virgin and this was the first time she had ever come. She lay now without stirring, her lips slightly parted, smiling and exhausted.

Grushenka studied her with curious sympathy; she knew the girl would not reciprocate and she let it go at that. Her own pussy could get satisfied only late at night when she stroked herself with loving fingers, thinking of her beloved Mihail.

Serge did not put her on his special list. He was much to busy trying to make money and to pile it up in his private iron chest. He loved to drink and gamble with the stable boys and he did not often feel inclined to get rid of his sperm. Whenever he felt in the mood he grabbed a few of the girls who were around, discarded the ones with fat arses and poked the others after his fashion. But Grushenka was to come into contact with him in another way.

One afternoon, cleaning the dining room, she was carrying one of the chairs with the big princely crown burnt into its leather back. Serge, running hurriedly through the room, bumped a leg of the chair with his knee. It hurt him and the culprit had to be punished on the spot. The leather whip was unhooked from his belt. Grushenka had to bend forward, put both her hands between her knees and was told to press her knees tight together and not to move. He ripped her blouse over her head. With his left hand he took hold of her hair, wrapping it around his wrist and the whipping began.

He raised the whip and flourished it over her. The stroke fell over her nude shoulders and the pain was worse than she had anticipated. It took her breath away and made her gasp. She uttered a loud shriek, writhing and twisting her loins in agony. He went on whipping her slowly, so that she felt the full sting of every stroke. It was as if a red hot iron was being drawn across her back and shoulders. She winced and squirmed every time the leather thong bit into her quivering flesh. She hopped around the room with her legs tightly together but that didn't do her any good. It only made him lay the strokes on in such a way that the end of the strap curled around her body and bit into her breasts, thus doubling her agony. She was about to faint or throw herself on the floor regardless of the consequences when he stopped. He kicked her in the behind and warned her to be more careful the next time.

When Grushenka, weeping and groaning, came back to her senses the other girls had gone. In fact they had quickly stolen out of the room when he took hold of her, because Serge did not mind whipping half a dozen backs once the mood was on him. They came back now and put sour cream over the long red welts which covered her back, shoulders and one of her breasts. It took days before Grushenka felt normal again and had forgotten the pain; it took weeks before the welts had disappeared.

It was a long time before Grushenka again came face to face with Serge. This happened when he sent word to the old lazy housekeeper to send him the six girls who had the best breasts. The girls did not understand what he had in mind and were thoroughly frightened. But they had to go to him. Of course Grushenka was one of the girls, who, clothed only in petticoat and naked from the waistline up, went to his room. They stood inside the doorway and waited. Serge sat over a big accounting sheet writing figures and cursing. Finally he threw the quill away, took a pinch of snuff and looked the girls over.

They all had full hard breasts, with white or brown skin, rosy or dark nipples. He had his choice. He got up, felt them, tickled them, weighed their full flesh in his hands and pinched them. They wiggled a bit and giggled but were uneasy. Naturally he decided on Grushenka. She had the finest of them all, milk white, full but pointed and with rather large rosy berries. He told her to go and put her finest dress on; a skirt and blouse but no shirt underneath. Grushenka hurried off to do so.

When she came back she saw him busy with the other girls. They kneeled in a row on the couch, bottoms in the air, one of them intruded by Serge's prick but probably all of them honoured with a few pokes because they comforted their behinds with their fingers or were tickling their pussies. He soon took his machine out of the hole which engaged it and went to the next crevice. Grushenka took care not to make any noise and not to be noticed in the doorway. She had no desire to give her behind this treat.

After Serge had come with his present incumbent, he gave every girl a slap on the arse and chased them all from the room. He put his prick quietly back into his trousers without troubling to wash it after his trip into the dirt holes, and turned to Grushenka. He opened her blouse in front, took her breasts out and tried to arrange the blouse so that the bust protruded well out of it. But it couldn't be done. The blouse was too large and had too many pleats, so that no matter how arranged the material covered most of the bust. He ordered the housekeeper to appear and demanded that an elegant evening dress be made for Grushenka but so cut in front as to go below the bosom. He smiled knowingly when he gave this order.

A light blue brocade, embroidered with silver flowers, was found in one of the many chests. This was duly cut and sewn into a magnificent evening gown. Grushenka helped and supervised this work eagerly. She knew from Nelidowa's tailors what was becoming to her and how a dress had to be made, and she looked very stunning when she presented herself a few days later to Serge. A bristling line of style and elegance ran through the whole creation; leaning back on a train, tightened together in a wasp-waist flanked by the long sleeves which trailed down to the knees and crowned by the absolutely nude bust which stuck out almost with impudence. Add to this that Grushenka had coloured her nipples with henna (as she had seen Nelidowa do); that she had her hair dressed in the high artificial style of the time and that she wore her most enchanting smile. Serge, the crude peasant and slave driver, could not help but admire and compliment her. Of course there was a great difference between Grushenka in a dirty working blouse, unkempt and half nude, and Grushenka fixed up as a great lady. More than satisfied Serge took her by the hand and led her to the room of the old Prince.

The old man shrank together and trembled fearfully when they entered the room and was about to hide under the covers of his large bed. His long hair was snow white and his white beard uncut. His small eyes were half closed, the eyelids red with inflamation. His nose seemed small and shrinking and the whole impression was of a Santa Claus who had met with an accident and lay frozen in the snow.

'Well here I bring you something fine,' began Serge, 'something that you will like, something to play with. And if you try to hide under the covers or to look away I shall hit you, you scoundrel. Didn't you always like the bitches with the big breasts, eh, when you were younger and I had to clean your boots? Sorry you are too weak or I'd make you clean mine now. Didn't I have to look on a thousand times, in those old days—when you put your pimply prick between their breasts—in those days when I always had to select the big breasted ones for you? Well you see I am kindly inclined now and bring you something to play with. Come on and feel it and suck it a little. It will do you good, won't it?'

The real reason for Serge's behaviour was that he had had enough of the old man. He wanted him to die but still shrank from the deed of killing him outright. His plan was to enervate the Prince still further. He hoped that the old man, after not having seen a woman for so long a time, would get excited and croak. Therefore he now pushed Grushenka towards the bed and the old Prince, trying to ward her off, could not help but touch her naked bust. This not enough, Serge pushed her over so that her breast lay on the Prince's face. But Serge saw that as long as he was present fear would occupy the old man's mind more than Grushenka's young bosom would excite him.

Sizing Grushenka up and finding her not dangerous, Serge decided to leave the two alone. He directed Grushenka to caress the old man's face every half-hour with her nipples, to let him play with her and to let him fuck her if he so desired. 'After the abstinence of so many years he is entitled to a little pleasure,' he remarked. With that he left them.

Grushenka sat modestly on the chair and watched the Prince. He lay still and stared stupidly into no-where. After a while she turned her eyes away from him, pitying him in her heart. She felt that he in turn was now scrutinizing her and before he could avoid it she caught a very keen and intelligent eye. So he was playing the old stupid man but was still very far from being demented! Finally he said in a low voice:

'You won't kill me, will you?'

'I'll pity you. I'll help you. I hate Serge'—was her answer. But they were both very careful not to say more; perhaps the serf who played the master was eavesdropping. After a while she got up and leaned over him as if to tease him with her breasts and whispered: 'I have to do this, he might be looking through the keyhole.'

The Prince played his part and stroked her bosom a bit. She noticed some books on the table and took one of them and began to read aloud. He was amazed that she could read and listened with interest to the story. But this interest grew to admiration when she inserted sentences into her monotonous readings which certainly were not printed in the book. For example, 'be very careful' or 'I must see you again' or 'make some plans of what to do' or 'when he comes back behave as though you never wanted to see me again' and so on.

When Serge came back to fetch Grushenka the old man complained in a stupidly wailing manner that she had got him hot and feverish, that he did not want to see her again, that she had disturbed him with her reading. Serge was pleased at this and felt especially gratified when Grushenka told him, after they had left the room, that the Prince was a delapidated old man, had no sense any more, and was certainly suffering from softening of the brain. Serge ordered her to make a daily visit to the Prince and annoy him more each time.

'Take his prick,' he said, 'or what is left of it, and rub it or suck it. Let him have a little excitement before he goes to hell—you are his serf anyway.'

At present, however, Serge wanted his own excitement quelled and Grushenka looked too beautiful in her full dress not to make an excellent partner. Right then and there her head was buried in the cushions of a couch while a sharp pain in her back-hole announced that Serge was still able to raise Master Prick into action. When he had thrown the long train of her dress over her elevated bottom and found a pair of drawers in his way he ordered her never to wear drawers again. He also decided that hereafter he would fuck her each day when she came out of the Prince's room. The dress of an elegant lady had stimulated his low-born senses and he ordered his other favourites also to be fitted with fine gowns to be worn when they reported for his pleasure.

Meanwhile Grushenka had to bear the brunt of his desire and she did so with the resolution that her revenge would not be far off. She had her arse-hole fucked again and again and surprisingly she very soon found it was not so terrible after all. On the contrary she learned how to loosen the muscles, how to

144

give herself easily, how to enjoy this reverse form of erotic excitement. Her only objection to her encounters with Serge was that he demanded she hold herself absolutely motionless no matter how aroused she became and how much she would have liked to answer his thrusts with wiggling pushes.

The liberation of the old Prince Asantschejew and the crushing of Serge came much more quickly than even Grushenka had hoped. She smuggled paper and pencil to the old Prince and, while she read to him, sitting so that a watcher from the key-hole could not see him, he wrote a letter. It took the old feeble man many days before the letter was ready and addressed. He had to hide the half-finished paper for days under his sheets, trembling for fear that he would be detected—and that would have meant a violent death from Serge's hand. Finally he slipped the finished document to Grushenka. It was addressed to a distant relative of his who had his castle in the city.

While Serge was in the house Grushenka, who had not confided in anyone, did not dare to carry the message herself to its destination. But one day when Serge drove away to watch the races she dressed hurriedly, ran out of the house, took a droshki and sped through the city. The relative was not at home, but his wife was. Grushenka forced her way through a chain of servants, came to the mistress, fell at her feet and poured out her story in great excitement. At the same time she delivered the letter.

At first the lady did not want to listen. Had not the old Prince sent them insulting letters some years ago asking them never to see him again nor to communicate with him again? Had not that dirty major domo refused her husband entrance to the house, acting upon orders from the old Prince? Had they not been shut out of his life entirely? How could he now expect to get help? But when Grushenka prayed hard to her she finally read the letter. She began thinking it over and had Grushenka repeat the story.

Then suddenly she understood; it became clear to her that Prince Asantschejew was actually the captive of his slave, that he had kept them away under the threat of death, and that they had to act. But how? She broke out in a flood of lamentations for with her husband away she did not know what to do. Yet Grushenka was in a terrible hurry. Action had to be taken before Serge came back, for he would strangle the old man upon the first suspicion. She suggested that they should get hold of some male acquaintances of Madame, and should get some men from the police station. But now Madame was calm again and took charge. She selected a half dozen of her strongest stable men and they drove at great speed to the castle of the old Prince.

Serge had not yet returned. The old Prince, upon seeing his relative, became hysterical, interrupting his joy with shouts of fear. Serge, whom he called an almighty devil, would kill them all, he proclaimed. His fear did not lessen even when they brought Serge before him, chained and shackled.

It had been an easy job. When he had re-entered the house, the six men of Madame had fallen upon him and subdued him in no time. A police-picket was sent for. In the presence of the lieutenant, the old Prince made his accusation against his serf and demanded that he be hanged. And so they led Serge away.

The captain of the police decided not to string him up but to send him to Siberia. But it never came to that. Serge, who had been stunned in the beginning, had a violent fit in the evening and tried to break loose. The answer was the knout and the policeman who exercised the whipping hit him so awkwardly that he broke his back.

Serge died during the night—this all can be read in the old family papers of the family Asantschejew. There also can be found that the old Prince gave Grushenka her freedom and a handsome dowry. He lived on for many months in peace and happiness. During this time Grushenka nursed him. After his death the relative who helped to free him inherited and lived in his castle—her name is reported as Countess Natalia Alexiejew. Grushenka stayed with the Countess Natalia until —well, the next chapter will tell you.

CHAPTER XIII.

Countess Natalia Alexiejew and her husband, the Count Vasilis, were Russian aristocrats of the old conservative order, a kind Grushenka had not yet met. They were religious, straight-forward, strict but just. They felt themselves the absolute owners of their serfs, but felt toward them more like a father or a mother than a master. Their day started early with a prayer meeting which was attended by the whole household, followed by breakfast at a long table, the masters presiding. If there was not a special party with guests, masters and servants ate at the same table and of the same dishes. After that, work was done.

Laziness or stupidity were at first treated with admonishing words. Only in rare and grave cases was the whip resorted to. The masters did not swing it themselves, however, but sent the culprit to the stable where an old and trusted coachman, named Joseph, laid the guilty one over a bundle of hay and administered the beating. Joseph was a Judas and beat them longer and harder than he was told to. The other serfs hated him. They took good care not to be remiss in their duties so as to stay clear of his fangs.

Furthermore, no erotic abuse took place in the household. The aristocratic couple shared the same bed throughout the year. The Count, who was past fifty, had lost his sexual aspirations, and the Countess, who was ten years his junior, was apparently satisfied with what he was able to let her have. She was nice and plump, with firm flesh and many pretty dimples. She had motherly ways, though always a bit preachy, and was beloved by all her servants.

A few weeks after the death of the old Prince she approached Grushenka and asked her what she intended to do. Did she want to leave her? Should she look around for a husband for her? Would she like to settle down on a little farm? What were her plans? Grushenka had no answer ready. After talking it over they decided that Grushenka should stay at the house for the present and the Countess put her in charge of the silver room.

Grushenka now carried on her belt a chain with many big keys which opened drawers and chests. She was proud to take care of countless sets of linen, from the coarse and daily-used bed linen of the serfs to the finest table damask, and of hundreds of pieces of china and many valuable silver ornaments which were put on the table on special occasions only. She had ten girls working under her, cleaning, repairing and sewing the new linen which had been woven by another group of girls or by the peasant women on one of the estates.

Her pride made her ambitious to have the utensils entrusted to her always at their very best. This ambition did not meet completely with the zeal of the girls working for her, especially in the beginning when they started to clean up after the years of disorder that preceded the death of the old Prince. She began to admonish her girls with friendly words, but she was timid and they laughed behind her back. It took all her courage to pinch one or the other on the arm, and she felt that as soon as she turned around they made faces at her and giggled. At last she complained to the Countess who gave the matter serious thought. She advised her as follows:

'The trouble with peasants,' said the Countess, 'is that they won't hear with their ears until they have felt with their backs. It won't do for you to report them to me and for me to have them sent to the stable. They'll only pin on you the stigma of a traitor and they'll think you're afraid of them and will play you plenty of tricks. No—you will have to keep some fresh switches in salt water in your working pantry. If you beat one or two of their backsides sore, they'll kiss the hem of your sleeves.'

After this advice, Grushenka got the switches and gave the girls a warning, but she made very little headway. The girls joked about the switches and broke the stems in the middle when she was not looking. There was one in particular, a big fat girl, about thirty years of age. She had been married twice to farmers, both of whom had died, and had always returned to the inner circle of the household because she had been one of the last favourites of the deceased Prince. She used to call Grushenka 'baby' and told stories about her married life which made the other girls stop working. She herself would do almost nothing in a day's time and when Grushenka pinched her in the arm, she would grin and say, 'Why, dear, do that again, please. It feels nice.'

She certainly did not feel it very much. She had a tough brown skin and the hard flesh of her peasant stock. Her overgrown, full breasts had first attracted the old Prince when he saw her once swimming in the river of his estate. She used to kneel down before him, put his penis between her breasts, press them gently together and rub until she felt his sperm flowing over her throat. She imagined that she had superior rights to Grushenka, hence her heckling and resistance. Therefore, when she aroused Grushenka's temper again and again, the supervising girl finally lost her patience and condemned her to twenty-five strokes over the bare bottom with the switch. The girl arose unmoved, took some hairpins out of her hair, and with them pinned her skirt up over her back. With slow movements and ceremony she removed her drawers, laid herself on the floor bottom up, and said sarcastically, 'Please hit me, sweetheart. I like to have a hot arse.'

Grushenka knelt with one knee on the back of the culprit and put the bucket with the switches next to her on the floor. In front of her was a tremendous arse; two big brown globes, muscular and steel-hard. The girl held her thighs closely together and strained her muscles in order to ward off the strokes. She was not at all afraid, because Grushenka was not very strong. Grushenka felt that if she did not beat the culprit into submission she would lose the respect of all her girls, and she pressed her lips together in anger.

'Open up you legs as wide as you can,' she ordered, curtly.

'Certainly, my dove,' retorted the girl mockingly, 'anything to please my little pet.' She spread her legs as wide as she could and at the end of the cleft appeared a great hole; a hair-infested cunt which seemed able to hold a big stick. The thick flesh on the end of the cleft was not muscular and the inside of the thighs next to the cunt attracted Grushenka's eyes. She directed the switch at those parts.

At first, being greatly excited herself, she laid the strokes weakly and swiftly. But when the girl did not seem to mind at all, even muttering flip remarks, she began to whip her with a force which she herself had not suspected she had. The flesh around the cunt became crimson; the first drops of blood appeared. The girl began to move uneasily. The ends of the switch were cutting the lower part of the lips of her pussy.

Soon the switch had broken to pieces. Grushenka picked a new one. Her hand got sore, but she did not mind. She was breathless, but she whipped and whipped, her eyes directed towards the end of the cleft and neglecting entirely the big, muscular thighs. Finally the girl felt the pain keenly. She had stood it at first to show up Grushenka and prove that she could not hurt her. But now the pain became too violent. She closed her legs. Grushenka, sensing victory and submission would not have it so. She shouted at her to open up again and when the girl did not obey, she bent over in a rage and bit her viciously in one of the big buttocks. The girl groaned and cried out, but reluctantly opened her enormous thighs again. This was not enough for Grushenka who jerked them open as far as it was possible and resumed her whipping, until the girl prayed for mercy and to be forgiven.

Grushenka stopped beating, but she was not yet through with her. She told the girl not to move until she had washed her up herself. In the hollow of her hand, she took salt water from the bucket and rubbed it into the raw, beaten flesh. The sting of the cold salt water shot up the girl's back, and as she instinctively recoiled, Grushenka manhandled her spot, pinching her all around the pussy and pulling its hair severely. Finally she inserted her sharp nails into the lips of the lovenest and with a last pinch, which made the culprit scream, let her go. After the girl rose, she gave Grushenka a strange look of mingled astonishment and devotion. She curtsied and kissed her sleeve, then went humbly to her work without wiping off the tears which trickled down her cheeks.

From that day her girls looked up to Grushenka with respect, and some of them even told her how glad they were that Grushenka had punished that bitch, who had been so fresh.

Grushenka herself had undergone a change by this experience. She now looked at her ten girls as her property and she enjoyed feeling that she could do with them what she wanted. She felt a certain thrill when she pinched their bare arms. She did not hurry when she had them expose the inside of a thigh or even a breast, so that she could squeeze the flesh slowly between the knuckles of two fingers, pinch hard, and twist her hand around. When her victim yelled or did not still, she did it over and over again, and she was aware that she got a thrill out of it.

She took even more advantage of her girls and they did not dare complain to the Countess. Grushenka had no lover, and her pussy often felt randy. What had Nelidowa done with her girls? For what had those lazy bastards their tongues? Remembering her one-time mistress, Grushenka had these girls suck off her cunt. The fat girl, who had been her antagonist, became her favourite for this sport. She had a long, crafty tongue and used to alternate rimming and tickling of the spot without being told to do so. But if one of the younger girls did not satisfy her, she beat her with a clear conscience. She used say to herself, 'Who had pity on me when I was in the same position?'

All this was erased by an event. The Count and Countess gave a great party. Grushenka supervised the serf girls in the handling of the dishes at the big buffet overflowing with food. Of a sudden there stood next to her—she had not seen him approaching—her Mihail. He was attired in gala uniform, smart from foot to head, young, alert, and in the best of moods. Grushenka only saw the bold blue eyes which had captivated her so many months ago. She stared at him as if he were a ghost and finally, understanding that he was really there before her, a guest of the party, she uttered a faint cry and turned abruptly to run away. He seized her and drew her toward him.

'Hello Mary!'—that was the name she had given him when he and his friend had picked her up on the road—'Hello, you mysterious lady. Don't run away. I have been looking for you everywhere. If you knew how often we discussed you, my friend Fladilow and I—he is still in Petersburg. We even made bets as to who you were. Now again I can't tell. You don't seem to be a guest, you're not wearing an evening gown, and you certainly are not a servant.' Grushenka wore a modish but simple grey silk gown and no wig.

'Let me go, let me go!' Tears dimmed Grushenka's eyes and she was all in a flutter.

At this moment the Countess passed and Mihail called her to his assistance.

'I can tell you all about my little brave friend,' said the Countess. 'She is a fine girl and very sweet too, isn't she?'

'We are old friends,' continued Mihail with a twinkle of the eye, 'but she does not like me any more. See, she wants to run away.'

'Please don't tell him anything,' pleaded Grushenka with her mistress. 'If—well, then, I'll tell him everything myself'—and she sighed so pathetically that they both laughed.

'All right,' consented Mihail, 'that will be much more to my liking.'

Grushenka took him by the hand and led him out of the room, away from the glamour of the thousand candles and the laughter and merriment of the aristocratic party. She seated him in a dark corner of one of the many pantries, and while the servants passed the room busy with their work, she poured a torrent of words out to him. She made herself as humble and miserable as possible. She told him that she was only a serf girl; that when he and Fladilow had picked her up, she was running away in the stolen clothes of her mistress, that she was a low, dirty creature not worthy even to speak with him.

When she was through, she burst into a stream of tears, embraced him and kissed him and clung hysterically to his neck, telling him that she had been liberated and was free now to go wherever she wanted and she would never separate from him again. Mihail understood only one thing of all this: that she loved him and had ceaselessly dreamed about him. She was very beautiful and in her tears she looked to him like a Venus. She felt that she pleased him and suddenly became normal again, quite reasonable in fact. She chided herself on being stupid, tidied herself up and smiled at him with great charm. He kissed her without passion, rather in a brotherly manner, and teasingly asked her whether she would sleep with him again. He promised her to be more polite hereafter, and not to snore. Saying he would see her again very soon, he went back to the feast.

The information he received from the good-hearted Countess was quite contrary to what Grushenka had told him. Of course the Countess knew nothing about Grushenka's past; in her good-heartedness and naiveté, she had not even a suspicion of Grushenka's previous adventures. She supposed the girl to be still a virgin, probably born of as fine parents as a free girl, but forced to sell herself into serfdom to ward off poverty. In liberating the old Prince, she had certainly shown great intelligence and courage, for if Serge had detected the plot, he would have tortured her to death. Jokingly she asked Mihail not to fall in love with Grushenka because she was no match for him. That they might start an affair did not even enter her mind.

But of course, that was exactly what happened—and how happy Grushenka was! Mihail, under the pretext of paying his respects to the Countess, had made good his promise and seen her again, and they had set a rendezvous. Grushenka slipped secretly out of the palace that evening and they took a long drive in his carriage. They had no intercourse that time, but loved each other like two good healthy young people. The next time, however, she went to his quarters, and they were passionately entwined on his bed before they themselves were aware of it. Grushenka, who felt heavenly thrills pass through her body when he only touched her hands, gave him her young body with all the passion and the strength she was able to muster. They loved and fucked and kissed each other until complete exhaustion overcame them. Mihail became almost more enamoured of her than she was of him. In fact, she soon became indispensable to him. They kept their meetings very secret and so enjoyed their happiness the more.

Summer was approaching. Mihail, whose full name was Mihail Stieven, had to go to one of the family estates which he administered for his father. He did not want to part from Grushenka. Naturally he conceived a bold plan to take her away with him as his mistress. Thus one morning the Countess received a very well composed letter from Grushenka who thanked her for her kindness and advised her that she had left for an unknown destination. The night before, Grushenka had smuggled all her belongings out of the palace and had left in a carriage with young Baron Stieven. They enjoyed all the happiness of an elopement.

The 'honeymoon' in the country was too wonderful for wordsd—at least Grushenka thought so as she silently said a prayer. In order to give her standing, Mihail had introduced her as his young wife and Grushenka was the 'beloved Baroness' and 'little mother' of her entourage. He should not have done that, as it turned out later on, but for the present his 'young wife' had a rosy time.

Grushenka, in her profound happiness, treated all the servants with great modesty and care. She was good to everyone, visited sick peasant women, brought food to their children, and the only quarrel she might have had with her beloved man was that he complained that she was too lenient and that she spoiled everyone.

She certainly spoiled him with her love. Nightly she encircled his muscular, firm body with her slender form. She gave herself to him without holding back anything, thrilling him to the core with the passion of her love. Not that she ever kissed his always excited love shaft; much as she wanted to, she did not want him to know that she understood anything about that kind of love-making. Not that she had caressed his balls or had even taken his privates in her soft hand. No, as soon as they lay naked in bed together, she beneath him, his tool would find the entrance by itself. But then she would practise her art—moving her buttocks in subtle circles, prolonging moments by forcing him to keep still when she felt that he was too near the climax, stroking his back with her hands and kissing his face and head over and over again.

Sometimes when he was already in bed and waiting for her

154

impatiently, she would tease him, hiding her pussy and her breasts with her hands, beguiling him by shaking her hips. When she came too near the bed, he would pull her in and it would take no time until she felt his beloved prick in her burning love-nest.

She learned to ride a horse, they drove around in his carriage, they took long walks, they discussed heaven and earth together. His admiration for her intelligence, quick wit and sound judgement grew steadily. He promised himself never to part from this girl, and she was immeasurably happy to feel the grip she had on him. They avoided visiting their neighbours lest the aristocratic landowners should be insulted with her presence. So perfectly did they seem made for each other that the future looked as bright as the present. They never discussed Grushenka's past life; Mihail did not want to know where she came from nor what she had done. She, on the contrary, wanted to know everything about him and he had to tell her his life from childhood on.

One day, after many kisses and goodbyes, Mihail left her to see a neighbour with whom he had to discuss grain prices and other things relating to the account he would have to make to his father about the affairs of the estate. He had been gone a few hours when the carriage returned with his coachman bringing her the message that she was to take the carriage and meet him at a certain place where he would ride on horseback. Gushenka had been sitting under a big chestnut tree in the garden, busy with some embroidery. She got into the carriage in her simple house dress without bothering to change or to take a hat. The destination named by the coachman was on the estate and not very far off. The coach drove with speed over the rough country ways. A few times the coachman turned his round, kind face back to her with a look in his eyes which she understood only afterwards.

After covering a few miles they met a huge travelling coach. The coachman stopped, so did the travelling coach. Two men stepped quickly out, jumped at Grushenka, bound and gagged her, threw her into the travelling coach and went off with her.

Grushenka was in a daze. Her own coachman, who

naturally should have defended his mistress, had not even looked around. There was no doubt about it, this was a plot. Her abductors put a kerhief over her head and resistance was impossible. The coach drove on for miles and miles. When the carriage stopped she was forced to get out, made to go up some stairs, bound to a chair, and then the kerchief was removed from her face.

She sat in a well-furnished room, apparently a room of an expensive inn. Her abductors left immediately, and she heard them report in the next room that she was safely delivered. Two elderly gentleman, well-dressed aristocrats, one with snow white hair, entered. They looked sternly at her, especially the older one, who scrutinized her with hard, unkind looks.

'So this is the vixen who has bewitched him,' he broke the silence. 'Well, we'll attend to her'—and such anger was in his tone that the other interfered.

'We won't make any headway that way,' he said. 'Leave her to me and everything will come out all right.' Then he addressed Grushenka, who sat anxious and fearful. 'Are you the wife of Baron Mihail Stieven? When and where did you marry him?'

'Who are you?' responded Grushenka. 'What right have you to ask me—and I am not his wife anyway.' She added this because she felt fear.

'Not his wife?' began the man again. 'Well, aren't you living with him?'

'I love him and he loves me and we can do what we want to, can't we?'

'Now look here, young woman, this is a matter of grave concern. This man is Mihail's father. Rumours have come to him that his son married secretly. Of course, he was interested in who his daughter-in-law was. Information came to us easily from the serfs of the estate. It's not Mihail's estate, remember, but his father's, and that is why the coachman abducted you today. We have also checked up on your past. That was not hard either. The Countess suspected that it was you who had eloped with Mihail. The girls told us that you had been bought through Mme. Laura, who in turn brought us in touch with Martha. She knew all about you. You are nothing but a run-away serf from the Sokolow estate. You've tricked the unsuspecting Mihail who is only a boy. He would not have lived with you as his wife if he had known that you were only a run-away serf whom we shall turn over to the police. Now confess when and where he married you and what priest performed the ceremony. We have means to make you speak,' he added threateningly.

Grushenka felt her hands get numb. She straightened herself up as well as she could and answered with dignity. She had never deceived her beloved Mihail, she had never married him, not even thought of it. He himself had given her a lift when she had fled from Mme. Sophia. She loved him dearly and knew very well that he was much too aristocratic and good for her. She was willing to become the serf of Mihail's father of her own free will, if only he would allow her to live near her lover.

Her words came unexpectedly to the elderly gentlemen. They seemed to be true and her arguments had weight. The two men had a lengthy discussion in French, which Grushenka did not understand. Mihail's father still seemed incensed, but the other man was more friendly. He proved this by cutting the strings with which she was tied without warning her not to run away. Finally Mihail's father spoke to her.

'I have other plans for my son and I will not allow you ever to see him again. That is final and he will acquiesce to it, because he does what I say. You can choose your own fate. If you are willing to make a sacrifice and stay away from him, I will take care of you. If not, I'll turn you over to the authorities, to Mihail's and your own ruin. For his mistress and bed-fellow will be whipped naked in a public place. You will be branded with an iron and sent to Siberia, as is becoming to a serf who deserts her rightful master. Take your choice.'

Grushenka cried. She cried for her lover. The men left her alone and locked the door. When the friend of Mihail's father came back to persuade her, he found that she had made her resolution. Of course she could not spoil the future career of Mihail. She was willing to give him up and when she was told that she could not even say goodbye to him, she acquiesced to that also. She was allowed to write him a letter and she put into her awkward hand-writing all the love and good wishes she had in her heart, telling him at the end that he should obey his father. Whether he ever received this letter is a question.

The men had supper with her in her room. She was unable to eat, but she managed to sit with them and to speak a little. They looked at her now with other eyes; they found her beautiful and enticing and the friend of Mihail's father remarked that he was punishing his son severely by taking such a lovely companion from him. But the old man remained firm and announced what her fate would be.

She had to leave Russia immediately. Travelling clothes would be provided for her, also her passport, and trusted servants would accompany her to the frontier. The Baron advised her to open a hairdressing salon or a gownshop with the ample money he would give her. Also that if she ever tried to get in touch with his son again, he would see to it that she'd die under the knout.

This was spoken by a man who had the power to do what he said and whose vengeance would surely follow her if she broke faith. Grushenka understood this only too well. Fate had taken happiness from her. She had been born a serf; the mighty decided her fate and her tears were not a weapon with which to fight against their will.

CHAPTER XIV.

Grushenka's trip through Europe is a history in itself, and cannot be retold here. She was young and beautiful, but sad. She had an abundant amount of money, or so at least it seemed to herself. She gave the impression of one of those travelling Russians so well known at that time for their unlimited orgies. Instead of settling down somewhere, she moved restlessly on until she came to Rome. This city impressed her greatly with its splendour and gaiety. With the Russian ability for languages she learned to speak Italian easily. She mixed with all kinds of company; with artists and students; with kept women, and now and then even with society.

After she had got over the blow which had struck her she plunged into countless love-intrigues. But she was always dissatisfied with the men or women with whom she went to bed, because her Russian strength and vigour surpassed the ability and appetites of her bedfellows. She indulged in utter sentimentality or brutal orgies. More than once she came into conflict with the police when she had aroused the neighbourhood in a drunken frenzy or beaten up her maids in true Russian style.

The whip was at that time in use all over the civilized world, but the Italian girls who now served her had a finer constitution than the Russian farmer-girls, and often fainted under her reckless tortures. Her good rubles, however, got her out of every scrape and 'the wild Russian girl' was soon a familiar figure in the by-ways of old Rome.

Drinking and gambling and whoring soon exhausted her purse. She took the ancient way out taken by all Eves; became a kept woman, ruining her lovers in a short time with her recklessness. Working for a procurer who catered to

159

strangers of the upper class, she again came into conflict with the authorities. As a result she fled to Nuremberg, which at that time had a flourishing Italian colony. But there she could find neither the customers nor the money which she had been accustomed to in Rome. She therefore married a humble German master-baker, but ran away from him without a divorce when his prick became exhausted after the honeymoon.

Meanwhile her longing to return to Russia had never ceased, and now—she was twenty-seven years of age—she made up her mind to go back. Her affair with Mihail, whom she still carried in her heart, would certainly be forgotten by both him and his father. She resolved to open up a modiste shop in Moscow—one like Mme. Laura had. She was adventuress enough now not to care where the money came from to start such an enterprise. Thus she stole what she could from her German husband, fitted herself out with an elegant travelling dress and, made up as a woman of the world, soon crossed the Russian border. To give herself a good front she carried many a big trunk, although they were filled only with stones. When she reached the gates of Moscow in a public stage coach, she got out and kissed the walls of the huge gateway. So happy was she to be back home.

CHAPTER XV.

The fat little innkeeper indulged in many bows as he showed Grushenka to his 'best room.' With many delicious phrases he praised Madame's beauty, admired her new Western travelling dress, humbled himself at the honour to be host to such a great lady. But his chatter was intermingled with hidden questions as to the private business of his new guest. Who were her family and relatives in the city, what was her status or occupation? The superficial answers he received were not to his liking. His curiosity had its origin in no personal dislike, nor did it come from anxiety as to whether he would be able to collect his bills. It originated in a very severe ukase of the police to keep an eye on lonely women and to report them at once to the authorities. This ukase had been created by pressure of the church in one of the clean-up actions which periodically befall all moral institutions.

Grushenka of course knew nothing about this. As she took her first stroll through Moscow's elegant streets and earned many appraising glances from the promenading gentlemen, she had every hope for a good harvest. At the same time the innkeeper sneaked into her room and inspected her belongings with knowing eyes. A locksmith soon notified him as to the contents of her trunks, and he crossed himself with a sigh. She seemed a nice lady all right but he did not care to go to Siberia for her sake. Harbouring an adventuress? No sir, better advise the police. This he did early the next morning.

Two big dirty policemen broke into Grushenka's room, while she was still soundly asleep. They did not listen to her protests, made her dress hurriedly, and not even allowing her to make up with care, drove her to the prison. A matron six feet tall and tough as the devil, suggested that Madame take her 'nice clean dress' off before she went to the dirty cell. She grabbed her garments with undue haste and slammed the door. There sat Grushenka in the half-dark cubicle, listening to the shuffle of feet in the busy corridors and the occasional yelling and crying of protesting women. What was its meaning, why did they lock her up? What had she done? She shivered in her bodice and petticoats and her unkempt hair fell down over her nude shoulders.

After hours of waiting two beadles called for her and led her before the district captain. He was a short man, with a round face and small piercing eyes, impatient to get through with his duties. He hardly looked at her passport and asked what the charge was. 'She's a whore,' said one of the constables, 'that's all.' Grushenka had not expected that. She had no story ready to answer this charge and being at a loss for an answer she spluttered out a lot of words to deny the accusation. The sharp question of the captain as to how she was living received the answer, 'on my money.' But she could not prove that she had any. When she said that she had just returned from foreign countries his suspicion arose even more.

'Maybe there is more about her than whoring,' he said. 'Maybe she is a spy or a member of one of those secret societies who wants to throw over our beloved Czar. Anyway, make her talk. Put her on the horse. She'll tell us all about it in an hour.'

The policemen dragged her away in spite of her shrieks and protests. They took her back to the prison and into the torture chamber. They beat and kicked her viciously. She found it better not to fight them and to keep still. 'That's better,' remarked one of them. 'Behave like a lamb and we will not bite you like wolves'—a joke which both of them greatly enjoyed. But they took no chances with her. They took her bodice off, removed her stays, tore the ribbon from her petticoat, which fell down by itself, and roughly removed her long trousers. They then tied her arms to her back with a strong cord. After that they took it easy and looked her over.

Grushenka's figure had changed greatly during her stay in Western Europe. Her fine, gracious form had filled out; she was plump and firm. Her bust, now moved sharply forward because her arms were forced back, was still of a marvellous firmness. The breasts stuck out without drooping, the waist-line was full and plump, the Venus Hill seemed enlarged and was covered with thick black hair, the legs were rather fat and soft. The most remarkable change, however, was in Grushenka's bottom. This used to be boyish but was now plump, full and womanly, and swung out from underneath the hips in two blooming buttocks. A woman in her prime stood between the two constables, her long black hair floating down over her shoulders, her blue eyes anxiously looking from one to the other and her full mouth imploring them to spare her. One of them, in a matter of fact way, took her full breasts and fondled them; she could not protect herself from his dirty hands with her arms painfully bound to her back.

'I think I am going to fuck her before we mount her up,' said he. 'She is the fairest of today's newcomers anyway.'

'Go ahead,' recommended the other one. 'Later on I'll take the small blonde in cell nine. I like the way she screams when I get her between me and her cot.'

'We can't dispute that,' was the answer. 'You like the young ones when they haven't got hair yet around the hole. I prefer the plump ones, like this'—and he slapped Grushenka between the legs over her woolly spot.

'I'll do anything you want,' wailed Grushenka. 'Everything! But please don't hurt me, I can't stand it.'

'We'll see to that later on,' replied the constable. 'Turn around now and bend over.'

She did as she was told. The other man, to help his comrade, went in front of her, took hold of her head, put it between his legs and closed his thighs, at the same time holding her up by the hips. The first constable had taken his big shaft out of his trousers. He grasped her big buttocks by their soft, thick flesh and moved them apart. He had no difficulty sticking his big prick into her lovenest. The entrance, once so small, was now wide open. Her cunt was juicy but the air of mystery was no more around it. Too many visitors had found pleasure in it and Grushenka's own passionate nature had helped to enlarge it. The constable took his time; there was nothing specially exciting in fucking a prisoner, especially one who was apparently a whore, and the men chatted while he worked away on her.

'Pretty big mouse trap,' said the one holding her between his legs. 'I hope you don't get drowned in it.'

'Better than a crack in the door anyway,' muttered the pushing man.

'Dust every nook and corner of it, will you, so that she'll remember you for a long time.'

'She'll do that anyway. There are no pricks where she is bound for.' Meaning the detention house where whores were sent.

'At least if you give her a brat they won't hang her,'—referring to the ancient law that a pregnant woman could not be executed.

While these and other remarks were heard in the room, Grushenka had her head buried between the high boots of the constable. The smell of grease and leather penetrated her nostrils. The dirt rubbed against her cheeks, and in her bent position the blood ran into her head. This was the first poke she received back on Russian soil.

How different she had expected it to be. Perhaps as the mistress of an aristocrat in a bed with silk sheets, or perhaps taking a young strong Russian into her own bed to be in the arms of a countryman again! Meanwhile one constable kneaded her full waist-line while the other one clamped his hands in the upper part of her thighs and fucked her with might. She remembered of a sudden that she needed the good graces of these men and she began to counter his pushes, to wiggle her arse with apt swinging and to embrace his love-shaft tightly. Just as she started, he came. She clasped her hands bound on her back, she tried to glue her pussy to his prick. But he took his instrument out in a matter-of-fact way.

Both men agreed she had a fine, softly upholstered bottom, better for the leather whip than for the knout. They slapped her soundly and let go of her. She straightened herself slowly, her face crimson and soiled with black from the boots. She implored them again not to hurt her. The men did not listen.

Orders were orders. They had to put her on the horse.

The horse was one of the oldest of torture instruments. Invented in oriental countries, it had been taken over by the Inquisition and thus spread all over Europe, it being one of the least expensive but most effective machines to be used on female captives. It consisted simply of a board nailed between four high legs in such a way that the narrow edge of the board was uppermost. The constables made her move towards it, forced her to step onto a little footstool and to swing one leg over the board into a sitting position. While one man held her from behind around the waist, the other one chained her feet together and put a weight on the chain. She sat now with her cleft over the sharp wood, the iron weight drawing the weight of her own body down. Placed as she was, she sat on her pussy and on her arse hole, which were the lowest spots on her body, and the sharp narrow edge of the lumber cut into her most sensitive parts. In addition, her jailers fastened a rope which hung from the ceiling through the cords which held her arms to her back. This made it impossible for her to throw herself forward or backward and thus relieve the pain of the pressure. Having arranged things properly, the men strolled out of the room, slamming the door without listening to her pleas that she would tell them all.

The first few moments it hurt her terribly, but she felt she could stand the pain. Then, of a sudden, a roaring pain shot through her loins and she began to scream in agony. She closed and opened her eyes, which rolled wildly. She cramped her hands together, piercing the nails into the palms. She tried to find another position which would take the weight from her tortured pussy. In vain. The weight on her feet and the rope at her back did not allow a change of position, and the more she moved the deeper the edge of the board intruded into her unprotected cleft.

She did not know how long she had been sitting in this cleaving, terrible position. Her screams became howls, the howling diminished to faint sobs. She was ready to lose consciousness, but the excruciating pain would not permit it. The police captain entered and, disregarding her sobbing pleas, took up a leather whip. The blows fell over her thighs, over her belly, over her breasts. They provided a climax of suffering; as the whip cut into her flesh, she jerked her body, thus adding to the horrible pains in her cunt. Yes, she was ready to tell everything—the truth, nothing but the truth.

The captain took the weight off her legs without removing the shackles, and tossed the footstool under her feet. She got onto it and stood with her sore spot only a few inches away from the terrible board; a push against the footstool would have brought her back to her former position. She told all; her whole life story.

The fat little police captain sat on a whipping block and listened. He scratched his head. This was a complicated case. He understood from her story that she was a liberated and free person all right, but on the other hand a runaway slave from the Sokolow estate. To whom did she belong now? To the Sokolows, to Mme. Sophia, or was the later liberation in force and was she to be considered a free person? He would not make a hasty decision on so complicated a question. In any event, for the present she belonged to the State, or better, to himself. Hence he would hold her until some enlightenment should come to him.

He left her standing over the board and went out. After a while, the huge prison matron came in. She took off Grushenka's chains and dragged her back to her semi-dark cell. The woman refused to give her back her finely made undergarments and left her entirely nude. Grushenka's protests were mild; while the pain had somewhat subsided, she felt so weak and sore that she could hardly walk.

Days went by in her dirty cell. The uncertainty of her fate weighed heavily on her, the noise and the screams throughout the busy prison got on her nerves, and the filth crept into her skin. One day the matron dragged her out, gave her a quick cleaning all over, dressed her in an old prison garb and turned her over to a waiting constable. He led her over many hallways and stairs, finally pushing her into the private room of the police captain. She paused, surprised, on the threshold. On the big table in the middle of the room sat a young whore. She was not older than eighteen, but one could see that she had been through much and was tough as leather. She was in her underwear and was engaged in a squabble with the undersized head of the almighty police department. He had no shirt on but was still in his trousers and made a ludicrous impression. Apparently he was as much pleased as annoyed with the impudence of the little creature who treated him like the dirt on her shoe.

'Hey you,' she addressed Grushenka, 'can you imagine that this big brute here claims that he is too good to kiss my pussy, my sweet little pussy mind you'—and she opened the slit of her trousers and brazenly held her hole open with both hands. 'I told him I wouldn't give him a thing unless it was thoroughly licked all over. He sent for you and claims that you ought to understand that job, at least if you don't lie to him—'

'All right,' grumbled the fat full moon, slightly annoyed, 'give her a Frenching. Perhaps that will make her keep still, brazen hussy that she is. But don't suck her until she comes or I'll beat hell out of you. I don't want to fuck a corpse.'

Grushenka stepped up and got busy on the vixen. Here was an opportunity to get her own fate decided; better make herself agreeable. She had learned to love to lick a cunt. Down in Italy she had often enticed young girls to come to her apartment, and she had got a thrill out of making them wiggle and scream under her tongue treatment. Often her maids had to hold them by force when they wouldn't give in. But she disliked this little whore and she could find no pleasure in sucking off her stinking hole, which, in spite of her youth, seemed to be well fucked out. She stooped down and opened her up in order to give herself a comfortable working position. The impudent street-trotter rested her body on the table and sent a triumphant look at the sturdy lover who fumbled about the room, and Grushenka's tongue began the operation.

This tongue had become broad and alert and knew its tricks from A to Z. The pussy, feeling that a master was at work, at once became intensely interested. The blonde creature had started this whole comedy only to tease her lover, but she discovered that—to her own surprise—a treat was in store for her and she decided to allow herself to come to a

167

climax. Grushenka felt how her clitoris, having swollen to hardness, suddenly fell together again. But she kept on licking so as not to have the police captain know that his love-partner was doing what he had forbidden: giving herself out before he put it in.

'Enough of this nonsense,' he interrupted Grushenka, and pushed her away. 'I'll give it to her now, whether she likes it or not.' With that, he shoved his short stub into the wet love-channel. Grushenka turned around, found a washbasin and cleaned her face. Then, looking at the couple, she decided she would not leave the room before she had cleared her own state of affairs with the captain. She saw him bent over the girl, his trousers around his ankles on the floor, his muscular buttocks busy with crafty pushes. An idea came to her. Swiftly she knelt down behind him, opened up his rim and glued her mouth to his back-hole. This had never been done to him. Surprised, he stopped his movements, and standing in front of his sweetheart, gave himself to this enjoyment. The girl, not knowing what was going on, called to him.

'Hey you, what's the matter? Getting lazy? Fuck me, you bastard! Fuck your sweet pussy!' And she heaved her bottom to get him working again.

He pulled the hair over her cunt roughly and his tone was so imperative that she listened in wonder. 'Hold still, you swine, and don't move, or I'll beat hell out of you—'

Grushenka caressed his balls with her fingers, tickled his dark hole with her tongue, and then inserted it. His legs trembled, he crushed himself against the young whore's thighs, groaned, and spent rapturously. Getting up to dress, the whore still wondered what had happened, but she guessed the connection when she saw Grushenka cleaning her lips with a wet towel, while her captain gave his testicles some gushes in the washstand. Grushenka found time now to plead her case with him. He kept thinking about it as a ticklish case. He told her to send the matron to him and with this decision, which meant nothing to her, she was led back to her cell by the waiting constable.

That evening the matron brought her his wise decision: as she did not belong to any private person at present, and apparently was not a free girl on the other hand, she belonged from now on to the State and was made herewith assistant to the matron. The deep thought of it was, of course, that he wanted her for his future pleasure and did not want her to die in that filthy cell.

The matron was very dissatisfied with this turn of affairs. She was, as Grushenka would soon find out, greedy to a horrible degree, and she was afraid that Grushenka might be an impediment to her doings. But she had to obey; had to give her some clothes, a living room next to her own, and had to put her to all kinds of tasks. Grushenka found herself busy preparing food—mostly a thin soup of nondescript contents—supervising the prisoners as they cleaned up their cells, and helping around in general.

Grushenka soon learned that there existed in the mind of the matron four classes of prisoners. First, those who had outside influence and were to be released soon and were not to be bothered. Secondly, those who had money and could get more from the outside. They were maltreated, but just enough to get more out of them. Thirdly, those who had money but did not want to part with it. They were mercilessly tortured. Finally, there were those who had no money or influence and were just left to rot away. She made no distinction in the age or state of health of the women she had under her thumb. She did not care at all whether they were criminals, thieves, whores, or poisoners, or whether they were innocent or picked up by mistake or on false and malicious accusations. They were only objects from whom to extort money, and she put the screws on them mercilessly.

As soon as they were delivered to her ward, she would take all clothes away from them and all money, jewellery, and other valuables. If it was an elderly whore or a woman who had been in the jail before, she would not hesitate to search even their cunts for hidden treasure. Then she would have them send messages through one of the constables to their outside friends demanding cash. If the money was forthcoming, the prisoner received a few days respite in the form of food and clothes and fresh air, the constable received a good tip, and the matron added more booty to her store. But woe if the message was unsuccessful! She would then give the unlucky one torture and Grushenka more than once had to assist her.

The torture chamber was there to extort confessions, as it was up to the middle of the 19th century in all countries of the world—although torture was officially abolished in most countries at the end of the 18th century. The matron, however, used the tortures to get her prey to come through. Furthermore, she did the job herself, and seemed delighted with it.

There was, for example, a big blonde woman about thirty years of age and apparently of means, judging from her wardrobe. She was brought in on a charge of shop-lifting, but it was patently a trumped-up charge because she was not brought before the captain for sentence. There was something mysterious about this woman. She refused to communicate with the outer world at all, and this was usually the one and only thought of other captives. She sat in her cell in dirty rags and moped without uttering a word. The matron dragged her to the black chamber, tore the rags from her body, and stretched her over the whipping block. The woman had a full, nice behind, a very light skin and shapely legs which instantly became the field of operation for her huge tormentor. Grushenka, who was supposed to help the matron, just stood around. The old and hardened jailer had not needed any help to tie her victim down, her strong muscular arms and her expertness in fastening the one strap over the middle of the victim's back, did not call for assistance.

'First I'll beat the shit out of you,' she shouted at the blonde woman, 'then we'll have a little chat.'

She made her word good. She began over the knees and hit the tightly stretched legs with all her strength with a switching cane. She went up one leg until she reached the cleft, beat the other leg the same way, and then let out all her rage over the buttocks. The woman was not muscular; she was of the finer type, well made and of soft flesh. She screamed in pain and swung her arms wildly, but was unable to shield her suffering backside with her hands. Blood-blue

170

welts appeared on her body. She wailed and promised to do everything. The huge matron stopped, but she dug her muscular fingers into the smarting behind.

'Will you write a letter to a friend or to your family asking for one hundred rubles to be given to the bearer?' Of course the woman consented.

She was led back to her cell and given time to sob to her heart's content, until Grushenka brought her a quill, ink and paper. The letter was duly sent away with a constable, but he came back saying that at that address there was no one of the name written on the letter. The matron got into a white heat. She did not say or do a thing that day. The next morning when she was through with her routine work, she again took matters into her brutal hands. This time Grushenka had to help carry the woman to the black chamber. She fought like a tigress and swore that the matron would be sorry, that she'd be beaten to death herself when she, the prisoner be set free.

Neither threats nor fighting helped her. The matron bound her hands to her back and pulled her up on a rope which was fastened to her wrists. This dislocated the shoulders, and the weight of the body, hanging on the twisted muscles of the arm, caused unbearable pain. The woman screamed that they were murdering her. Grushenka, who herself was no longer soft hearted, felt pity. But the matron did not seem to hear nor to have the slightest compassion. She tied the woman's ankles in a far-outstretched position to some rings in the floor, thus bringing still greater pain to the shoulders.

Grushenka looked at the hanging figure. The twitching face was not beautiful, but still had good-looking features. The breasts, too large and too full, drooped, but the belly was flat and without fat. The best parts were, without doubt, the firm, shapely thighs. Grushenka could not help stepping close up to the woman and studying her, even feeling the cunt which was wide open, due to the outstretched position of the legs. It was a cunt and not a pussy all right, which means that the hole was large as to entrance and sheath. The woman was strung up so high that the vulva was exactly at the height of Grushenka's mouth, and she could not help making a sarcastic remark. While fumbling around with her fingers, she said to the matron, 'I guess she has opened her legs so wide for a sucking, don't you think so?' But the matron, who had meanwhile carefully looked for a knout, pushed her rudely away.

'You'll see what I'll give her, and as you call my attention to her spot, it's a good suggestion. I'll let her have it there.'

The knout, a short wooden handle to which were fastened eight or ten short leather straps, began its work. Standing alongside and at an angle to her victim, the matron began slowly and with precision to beat her. She directed the end of the leather straps at the cunt and at the surrounding flesh on the inside of the thighs. She did not count the strokes, she did not hurry. She took good aim, swung her arm out and—swish—the blow crashed into the most tender parts of the hysterical, screaming woman. Not so many blows, only ten or twelve, because suddenly the woman became pale and her head dropped down. She had fainted.

The matron released her leisurely, slung her over her shoulder as if she were a bundle of clothes, and threw her roughly on the cot in her cell. When weeping was heard from that cell, the matron looked in on the prisoner again. The woman consented to write another letter, but the outcome was far from what the matron had expected. The constable stayed unusually long and when he came back there was a distinguished-looking man with him who had a release for the prisoner. He swore by heaven and hell that he would get even with the matron when he saw the state the woman was in, and left with her in a hurry. The matron only shrugged a shoulder. Let them complain. Nothing would come of it, even if the Czar was their cousin—and she was right.

Punishments were not usually so cruel, unless the object was to make a prisoner speak. Very often, however, the captain, sitting as judge and jailer at the same time, ordered a beating on general principles when a woman had to stay in prison only a few days for a minor offence. These minor offenders were not sent to the State prison nor brought before a jury, but did their time, mostly less than a week in the police prison. Such cases were handled similarly to the following,

172

which was entrusted to Grushenka.

Two young whores, hardly sixteen years of age, had been picked up soliciting in the streets. Women were permitted to do that, but only during certain hours of the evening and on certain avenues. Perhaps these girls, who were friends, had sought to make a better haul in the lighter main-streets; anyway, they had become the prey of the law and were each sentenced to five days in jail. As an added punishment, they had to sit every morning for one hour in the stocks and to receive twelve strokes with the switch.

The girls had no money and were turned over by the matron to Grushenka. At first they cried bitterly, but having a cell together, they began to make plans for the future almost before they had started to do their time. They were more curious than afraid when Grushenka led them to the black chamber. They took their clothes off meekly and climbed by themselves into the stocks. Grushenka used only the hand and foot stocks on them, not the head stocks, and she saw to it that the boards did not crush their skin. They sat next to each other on the floor, hands and feet close together through the boards. They did not seem to mind that their bare behinds rested on the hard stone floor. They were good-looking girls, joking with each other and teasing each other that their lean arses had to carry their whole weight. They had small, round breasts and there was something young and fresh about them.

Grushenka, who for a long time had not had a good party for her pussy, got slightly hot. She bent down and teased the girls' nipples and was curious about their pussies. But they pressed their thighs close together and said, 'No, Madame, it costs fifty copecks to make us open up; that's our price.' Grushenka suggested that they suck her pussy a little; they claimed that they did that to each other and could not be untrue to each other. But if she would promise not to give them the switch—. Grushenka said she would have to beat them a little in order to make some marks lest the matron should interfere, and they agreed on that.

Grushenka let them out of the stocks, sat herself on the whipping block, and had one girl kissing her pussy while she

173

got hold of the other one. Kissing her with rising passion on the mouth, she licked her teeth and tongue, and began to feel her up. Moving her hands down to the girl's behind, Grushenka first fingered the pussy a little. This the girl did not mind. Then with passion she began to feel around the little dirt-hole. But to this the girl did not agree. She moved her behind out of reach of Grushenka's hands, which so much more wanted to feel the perversely erotic little spot. Grushenka, however, spent before she succeeded. But she kept it in mind.

She had the girls hold each other in turn over the other's back and laid some six strokes over each behind, just stinging the skin a little. When she was through the girls laughed and protested that they could stand more than that.

The next morning Grushenka used the head-stocks on them. In these the prisoner stood erect and had to put his head and his hands through openings, which were closed by boards laid on top of them. Having secured them that way, Grushenka went leisurely around the stocks and began to pinch and fondle their naked bodies. Finally she shoved a finger of her left hand into the pussy of one of the girls and took possession of her back-hole with the index finger of her right hand. The girl kicked and shouted and moved around uneasily, but was, of course, unable to avoid this treatment.

'You must get used to it someday,' smiled Grushenka. 'You will soon enough feel bigger things than that move in and out—some men like it only that way.' And she gave the girl a long finger-fucking while she thought of the many Italian men, handsome too, who had taught her to come with the same ease whether the prick was in the front or in the back entrance. But the girl disliked the rubbing finger thoroughly and protested that she never, never would stand for that. When Grushenka applied the same playful method to the other girl she had a surprise. This girl was seemingly satisfied with it.

'You see,' explained the girl, 'it is this way. Next to my father's store there was a cobbler, who was the first man to make love to me. At first I had only to take his shaft in my hands, but then he wanted better things. He was afraid to make me pregnant. I was only fifteen then, mind you, and he did not dare to put his machine into the right place. So he fucked me in the back. That was the first time I ever had a prick in me. I screamed a bit, not too much because I was afraid of detection, and then got used to it. So rub me there a bit, I don't mind—' which of course made Grushenka desist from doing so.

While this and other things went on, the captain made use of Grushenka for his purposes quite often. Any time his impudent sweetheart came to see him, he had Grushenka go down on his back. But he did not allow her to suck off the little whore again, and she in turn was angry at Grushenka's presence. A few weeks passed by, until one day she openly rebelled and refused to let him have her as long as Grushenka was around. He swore at her and beat her, but she answered with not less flowery words and hit back. All the while his prick stood at attention.

Grushenka, seeing the row, had an inspiriation. Tearing her clothes off, she got a sudden hold of the captain, encircled him in her arms, and drew him and herself to the carpet. Before the astonished man knew what it was all about, she had her thighs around him, his prick in her pussy, and she was fucking him with the circling movements of her hips. He was really worked up and soon answered her thrusts. An amazing encounter started. The girl, first believing Grushenka was going to help her, then suddenly realizing that she was fucking her own lover before her eyes, got enraged and tried to pull the two away from each other. She rolled them over the carpet, kicked and pushed them, tore at their limbs, punched their backs and kicked them in the behinds. But they were so hotly involved that they continued fucking in the face of this bodily aggression—were even stimulated by it. They groaned in the climax. It was a magnificent experience.

The captain got up first, while Grushenka lay with closed eyes, exhausted on the floor. The captain was now really furious with his former bed-fellow. He let her have it in words and blows, and threw her out, never to come back. Grushenka got up slowly, softly embraced the man, whose rage was just

175

ebbing away, and kissed him tenderly on both cheeks. The fat little captain, who had not been kissed in this way in years, and who had just detected what a rare poke Grushenka was, softened to a degree which was unusual with him.

'No use,' he muttered, 'to have you out in the ward all the time. I'll tell you what we'll do. You become my housekeeper from now on.'

He lived in comfortable quarters in a wing of the prison, and Grushenka moved in. She was more like a dutiful wife than a housekeeper and lover. She cleaned and cooked for him, made his private life comfortable, satisfied his sexual desires with prudence, never overworking him, and saw to it that he always wanted her. He in turn treated her quite like a human being. He took her out with him in his carriage, introduced her to his friends, never beat her, and was satisfied to be henpecked. Months went by and Grushenka was undecided whether she should make him marry her. Why not? He had plenty of money and a position of a kind, and she would have a certain security. But finally she abandoned this idea.

CHAPTER XVI.

The reason Grushenka did not want to be coupled for her lifetime with the captain of the police was, no doubt, inspired by her physical aversion against him. He was round and fat, his arms, backside, legs; everything about him was stupidly rounded and unpleasantly self-satisfied. He was not a good lover and when, once or twice a week, he put his short and stubby shaft into her sheath and gave himself a good rubbing in her, without considering her desires, he felt well pleased with himself. He snored in bed, he did not believe in keeping himself clean, and he spat in the room as one might have done in a pig-sty. He exercised his duties brutally, and his means to justice was the whip. Even his jokes were vile, so why stay with him?

In order to break away, Grushenka needed money and she had none. The captain, however, had plenty. In the evening his pockets were always bulging with gold and silver; yet he left in the morning without a cent. The bribes he received were enormous. But what did he do with his money? Grushenka found out quickly enough. He had a big iron cash-box, standing on the floor, about three feet high and five long. There was no lock on this box but it would not open for Grushenka. She watched him and saw him move a little handle on the back of it. The next morning she lifted the lid and was amazed. The box was filled almost to the top with thousands of coins; gold, silver and copper. He had thrown them in carelessly, as they came his way.

Grushenka did some thinking. She then proceeded to rifle his pile of wealth systematically. Every day, while he was away, she helped herself to a few hundred rubles in gold. Of these she changed one or two pieces into silver and coppers and threw them back into the box so as not to leave any holes.

The rest she kept. Soon she had accumulated many thousand rubles, without the pile of coins having become smaller. She transferred her treasure one fine day to a banker—it was enough for a good start.

All that was now left was to get away from the man. This she accomplished through weeks of careful manipulation. First she became apparently moody and sickly and wailed about her failing health. Then she refused to have him when she felt that way. Of course he would not stand for that, but mounted her against her protests. While he worked away on her, she would start a conversation with him, annoying him all the time by talk. She would ask him to come quickly or, out of a blue sky—when he was ready to come—would ask him what he wanted for dinner the next day.

Of course he in turn did not treat her too kindly. Often he would give her a sound slap, providing her with a good excuse for a sulking. Once or twice he turned her over and spanked her bare behind with his hands. She stood it because she knew he would soon want her to leave him. He began to fuck his prisoners again, as he had been in the habit of doing when he had no whore who enticed him. She would hear, of course, that he was untrue to her, and would make scenes about it.

Simultaneously she spoke with him about the disorderly houses in Moscow, how excellent that business was, and how little the bribes were that he collected from them. Soon she approached him directly as to whether it would not be a good idea for him to run a whore-house himself, give it his whole protection, close all the other ones and—put her in charge of it. He would not listen to it, because he was not interested in money after all. But when she painted, in the brightest colours, how he would be master of it, how she would always provide him with very young girls who would put on great parties for him, he succumbed to her wiles and told her to go ahead and do what she liked. But she was to understand that he had no money whatsoever and that she would have to put the house on its feet by herself. She almost loved him for that and got busy at once.

Grushenka acquired a house in the best neighbourhood,

where without the captain's protection, nobody would have dared to open an establishment of this kind. The house, surrounded by a small garden in the front and by a large one in the back, consisted of three floors. The upper floors contained about a dozen rooms each, while the ground floor had a magnificent dining room and four or five very spacious drawing rooms, all leading to a big front hall. Grushenka modelled the whole mansion after the layout of the best whore-house in Rome, which she had visited quite often to get her pussy kissed.

She resolved that it would be best for her to employ only serf girls, who she could train for her purposes without having to consider their wishes. She prepared all this without the captain's knowledge. And she had to make more raids on his cash-box, because she furnished her establishment with the best. There were a colourful carriage and four horses, a few stable men, an old housekeeper, and six sturdy peasant maids, lovely furniture, and of course, a well-selected choice of four-poster beds with canopies and silk sheets. All this assembled, she left the captain, settled down in the big house and began leisurely to buy her girls.

We see her now, going in her own carriage, to all parts of Moscow, looking over features and shapes the way Katerina had done about ten years before, in order to buy her for Nelidowa. But she had it easier than Katerina because she did not have to look for any special type of girl; she needed girls of all types and shapes to satisfy the taste of her prospective customers. The hunger in the poor sections of Moscow was responsible for her best finds. Not only foster-parents, but also parents, would flock to her with their daughters. The girls, on their part, were delighted to enter the services of so fine and elegant a lady, where they would be safe from starvation.

Grushenka would send word through her housekeeper to one of the poorer streets that she was willing to buy a few young girls, between fifteen and twenty years of age, for her private service. She would be told where, for example, in the backroom of a certain inn, she could look over the merchandise. When her elegant carriage rolled into the street, there would be great excitement, the mothers flocking around her, kissing the hem of her garments and imploring her to take their daughters. After the near-riot of her arrival was over, Grushenka would be led into a large room, filled with twenty to thirty girls, all in rags, dirty and smelly. The chatter and shouting of the parents, anxious to sell, would make it impossible for her to select at ease. The first few times she was so helpless against all this, that she left without making an attempt to look the girls over. Throwing alms on the ground for which the mob scrambled gave her the opportunity to leave quickly. But then she found a better way; she removed all the parents from the room, resolutely locked the door from the inside, and went about her task in a business-like way.

The girls had to throw off their rags. Those she disliked she sent from the room, keeping the three or four who seemed likely. She submitted these to the most rigorous examination. Long hair, beautiful features, perfect teeth, well-formed bust, and small juicy cunts were not the only requirements. She wanted girls who showed vitality and strong resistance. She took them over her lap, she had them open up, she played with the tickler and watched the reaction. She pinched them with sharp nails on the inside of the thighs, and when they showed any softness she gave them a couple of coins and sent them away. For those she selected, she made a hard bargain, clothed them in garments she had brought for that purpose, and took them right away with her.

After a meal and bath in her mansion, she administered the first whipping herself. She took this very seriously. It was a further try-out as to whether the girl was to make good. She did not take them down to the black-chamber, which she had found in the house when she had bought it from an aristocrat. Nor did she tie them. She put them on the elegant bed which would be theirs for the love-business later on, and under the threat of sending them back, made them expose those parts of their bodies she wanted to hurt with the whip.

All of the girls had been beaten before, but they had mostly received rough blows and kicks and few of them had been submitted to a skilful whipping by the leather whip. After laying stinging blows on their buttocks and between their thighs, she would make them get up, stand erect, and order them to hold their breasts from underneath ready to receive punishment. Those who complied were not touched at all, but those who were not ready to follow this order, would feel the whip again and again on their backs, until complete submission was affected. Grushenka had lost her softness; she had forgotten the fear and terror of her own youth. And this made her a success.

When she had collected in this way about fifteen girls, she began careful instructions on how to keep the body clean, the nails in perfect shape, how to smile and to walk, how to eat and to talk. She succeeded quickly, especially because she had the most magnificent clothes made for her charges, and fine clothes inspire every woman to refined behaviour. Satisfied with this she also gave them special and delicate instructions in how to handle and satisfy the men, instructions which, if repeated here, would make a whole chapter by itself. She spoke to attentive but bewildered girls. They heard the words but did not get the meaning in full, for it turned out that one-third of her fifteen girls were still virgins. If they had been fucked previously at all, they had just lain still when the rough men of their sections were working in their pussies. They did not understand yet how there can be a great difference between an expert courtesan and a peasant girl who just holds her legs open. They should know better soon.

When Grushenka felt she was ready, she held the great and boisterous opening of her establishment. According to the custom of her time, she had an invitation printed which was quite a document, prettily lithographed and adorned with vignettes displaying love scenes. Here you could read that the famous Madame Grushenka Pawlowks, just returned from an extensive tour over Europe in search of new and never-dreamed-of sex excitements, was inviting the Honourable Dukes, Counts and Barons for the great opening of her establishment. Here the customer, from the moment that he passed the threshold, would be drowned in an ocean of pleasure, etc ... etc ... followed by the most startling announcement, namely, that for the opening gala banquet,

181

no charge would be made! On this night, every one of the famous beauties would satisfy every whim free of charge, and a free lottery would be played, the prizes being five virgins to be raped by the winners!

Here—according to the style of the time—a special specification was also made, that the winners could deflower their prizes either in private chambers or 'in state'. It must be known that most marriages of that time started with deflowering 'in state', which means that the bridegroom put his prick into the little pussy in the presence of all the near relatives, often all the wedding guests, in order to give a proof by witness that the marriage had been consummated. This habit flourished in the families of reigning houses of Russia right through the better part of the 19th century.

The opening party turned out to be a riotous bacchanal. It lasted not only one day and one night, but more than three days and nights, until it was finally disbanded by the discreet and quiet interference of the police. Grushenka received the guests in a gorgeous gown, very audacious, as was becoming for this occasion. From the waist down she wore a purple brocade skirt with a long train which encircled her in gracious swirls wherever she went. From the waist up she had on only a thin silver veil, which left her magnificent breasts and full rounded back bare to the view of the admiring men. She wore a large white wig with many curls which, because she had no diamonds at that time, was adorned with dark red roses. Her girls wore smart evening gowns which just left the nipples free and which were close-fitting in the waist but wide around the hips and behind. They had no undergarments on whatsoever and while the men were eating, Grushenka introduced them on a platform, one after the other, lifting their gowns up in front and in the back, displaying and covering up their undercarriages from ever angle.

Grushenka had counted on about seventy visitors. Over two hundred came. Two oxen had been slaughtered and had been roasted in the garden over an open fire, but she soon had to send out for more food. The battalion of bottles of wine and vodka drunk during those days will never be known. A small army of hired lackeys were busy opening bottles and piling empty ones in the corners.

The first feature after the dinner was the lottery for the virgins. After long, and more rowdy than witty speeches, the men decided between themselves that anyone who would not 'fuck in state' should be excluded from participation. The men were all from the aristocratic class, mostly landowners or their offspring, officers of regiments, government officials, and so on. But they were drunk and found that this was one occasion to break down barriers.

They cleared a space in the midde of the great dining hall and herded the five young girls into the middle, where they stood sheepishly. Numbers were hung around their necks, and every man received a numbered card, the winners being those who held numbers corresponding with those of the girls. The girls were now told to slip out of their dresses, while the winners proudly stood next to them. The rest of the crowd lay, sat or stood all around the room in a circle. Some had climbed to the window sills to see better. The girls were frightened and began to cry. The crowd answered with cheers and boos.

Grushenka stepped into the circle and got her wards close together. She spoke to them with quiet determination, but threatening them if they did not cheerfully obey. They slipped out of their gowns and lay meekly down on the carpet, closed their eyes and kept a hand on their pussies. But their ravishers found themselves also in a predicament. Two, it is true, had nice hard shafts when they opened their trousers. The other three could not so quickly find the trick of how to raise an erection in this noisy crowd. They discarded their coats and opened their trousers and lay on top of their girls all right, but good intentions don't mean a job accomplished.

Mme. Grushenka stepped into the breach. She devoted her services at first to those two who had their guns ready to fire. Soon enough a piercing cry came from one of the girls and the struggling of her bottom announced that Mme. Grushenka had, with her apt fingers, put the prick of her first customer into a love-nest. The second outcry came soon afterwards.

With the third one—the shaft belonged to a young lieutenant of the cavalry—she had more difficulty. While her left hand tickled his cleft, her right hand massaged his balls and sword so cleverly that she soon inserted it into the sheath.

Number four proved a futile attempt. The gentleman in question was more than anxious, his prick was full but flappy. As soon as Grushenka touched him he gushed into the air and over the hairy Venus Hill of the little bitch underneath. When he got up, crimson in face and ashamed of his misfortune, the watching crowd did not at first understand what had happened. When they finally did, a bedlam broke loose. Of course, a substitute was quickly found and the maidenhead of numbers four and five were duly pierced.

For a moment the half-clothed men lay heavily breathing on top of the nude white forms of the girls whom they covered. The heavy air in the room was filled with rankness. Each fellow, after the climax, got up and proudly exhibited his throbbing prick covered with blood. Grushenka had a devilish time getting the freshly deflowered girls safely out of the room. She had to fight through the crowd of men who clutched and pawed the scared girls on whose thighs were smeared the blood of their rape. Grushenka turned them all over to the old housekeeper who administered to them in a room on the third floor.

When Grushenka came back, she got into another mêlée with the excited men. They wanted to auction off the other girls also. A suggestion came from some corner demanding another maidenhead, namely that of the backhole. Grushenka did not want to hear anything about that and tried to joke them out of it. They started to manhandle her and as she was about to leave the room, tore the thin veil, even her wide skirt, from her, so that she was left only in her lace pants. They crowded in on her, half good-heartedly and joking, half threatening. She became frightened and promised everything.

She reached her ten remaining girls who were waiting in a room upstairs to hear what was demanded of them. She made a resolution to bundle them all in a carriage and to hustle

184

them out of the house, leaving the drunken men to get sober and to disperse. But on second thought she remembered how dependent she was on the success of this event. Her very last money had gone, even the house having been mortgaged to provide the food and the wine. Furthermore, it might be good to let the girls get some rough treatment from the start. They would not be the worse thereafter. She had them take their gowns off before she marched them into the room where the men waited impatiently. She did not care that her wig was crooked on her head and that she had only her trousers left to cover her body. She was now all energy, resolved to play the game, and to do it in great style.

The men behaved well when she brought the girls in nude. They had put ten chairs in a circle in the middle of the room and had arranged for a complete lottery which took some time to carry out. Meanwhile they stared at the ten naked beauties in their midst. Many randy comments and jests flew through the air. The girls in turn, stimulated by Madame and not knowing what was in store for them, answered the men with no less cheery remarks. They threw them kisses, touching their lips, and then their breasts or cunts in salutation to the fellows who, they said, they would like to win and get poked by.

The winners decided on, Grushenka picked out for every group two helpers who should stand by and give assistance. The girls were told to kneel down on the chairs and to hold their arses in the air ready for aggression. They did so laughingly and opened up their knees, for of course they thought they were going to be poked in the pussy. It was a wise move of Madame's that she had selected those helpers. They now stood alongside each couple, held the girls' heads down, played with their nipples and made excursions towards their ticklers. It was lucky because every one of these simple girls, as soon as she felt that the prick tried to force her backdoor, howled and began fighting. They jumped from the chairs, rolled over the carpet, kicked with their legs, and were utterly inclined to put up a good fight.

And how the watching crowd enjoyed it! Bets were made on who would be the first man to succeed and who would be the last girl to be arse-fucked. None of the men had ever seen such a spectacle and the party became a huge success. The gladiators took their pricks in their hands and rubbed them quite openly. Self-restraint or shame was by now entirely lost. Grushenka herself, standing in the middle of the circle, was caught by the atmosphere and if the men had demanded that the girls should first be whipped, she would have agreed to it gladly—for her own pleasure as well as that of her guests.

The girls were overpowered in different positions: some lying on the floor on their belly, others with their heads between the legs of a helper bending over them, one in such a way that the man sat on a chair while the two helpers put the girl on his lap, holding her in the air by her knees so that she could not stave off the attack.

Only one girl was still fighting on the floor, a small young girl, very blonde, her long hair loosened and dishevelled over her bust and shoulders. Grushenka stepped in and settled the matter herself. She waved away the man whom the girl had each time skilfully shaken off at the moment when he thought he was about to succeed.

Grushenka made the girl get up and took hold of her by the hair between her legs and by one breast. Hypnotizing her by putting the whole weight of her personality into a few commanding words, she subdued the girl completely. She made her kneel on the chair and bend very low. Then she opened up the cleft and cleverly fingered the tight arse-hole for a few moments. She now invited the winning man to come and take what was his. The girl did not stir and did not dare to make an outcry when she felt her back-entrance filled with a big love-instrument. She was, incidentally, the only girl who got fucked kneeling on a chair in the way the men had intended it for all of them. But none the less, every one of them lost the innocence of their back-parts.

When this spectacle was over, Grushenka ordered every girl to go to her room and to wait for visitors. She invited the men, after the girls had left, to go into the rooms and to have a good time with the girls. She computed that every girl would have to take care of about ten men, which they could do very well.

The men did not ask for a second invitation, and went not alone but in groups, friends and strangers together, just as it happened. For the next few hour some fellows were sitting in every girl's room. While one man lay on top of a beauty who wiggled her bottom strenuously in order to get through as quickly as possible, others were waiting their turn.

If the men had gone home afterwards, as Grushenka had planned, everything would have been fine. But after shooting their sperm, they returned downstairs and lay and sat around, drinking. Songs filled the air, jokes were told, glasses were emptied, food was devoured. Some slumbered for a while only to wake up ready to begin again. After they had beguiled themselves enough downstairs, they would explore the whole house again watching the fucking and mixing in it themselves.

Many scenes of lust and depravity took place in the girls' chambers. One group of fellows, for example, remembering the deflowered vigins, broke into their rooms and let them have some arse-fucking, in spite of their tears and protests.

Grushenka was everywhere and anywhere, first animated and cheery, then weary and tired. She slumbered in an easy chair, took a drink or two again, comforted her girls, or got drunken men out of the way. Finally she sent a lackey to her captain, who tactfully succeeded in getting the drunken guests out. The mansion was in a state of disorder and dirt. The tired-out whores and their mistress slumbered in a deathlike sleep for forty-eight hours.

But the excitement, costs, and lasciviousness of the strenuous task had not been for nothing. Madame Grushenka Pawlowks had put her establishment on the map, and she handled it afterwards in a spirit very much to the advantage of her purse. She became rich and famous. In fact, so much so, that after her death and after her famous salon had long been closed, anyone in Moscow could point out her house, just as in Paris is still pointed out the famous establishment of Madame Goudan, who one hundred and fifty years ago was known all over Europe as the best Madame in the world, under the pet name, 'the little Countess'.

How Madame Grushenka ended up her own love life is not

known. It might be that she found her satisfaction through the aid of the friendly tongues of her girls; maybe she married a solid young man to whom she clung quietly without the public's knowledge. The last time that we hear of her is in an official police document where she is described as 'a distinguished lady in her prime, well formed, and refined, with bold blue eyes and a full, smiling mouth, which is able to talk adroitly and to the point'. May this description of her have been fitting to her until her

END.